Onitsha

J.M.G. Le Clézio

Onitsha

Translated by Alison Anderson

University of Nebraska Press, Lincoln and London

Publication of this
translation was assisted by
a grant from the French
Ministry of Culture.
© Éditions Gallimard,
1992. Translation © 1997
by the University
of Nebraska Press
Library of Congress
Cataloging-in-Publication
Data. Le Clézio, J.-M.G.
(Jean-Marie Gustave),
1940– [Onitsha. English]
Onitsha / J.M.G. Le
Clézio: translated by
Alison Anderson. p. cm.
ISBN 0-8032-2915-1 (cl :
alk. paper). – ISBN
0-8032-7966-3 (pb : alk.
paper). I. Anderson,
Alison. II. Title.
PQ2672.E2505513
1997   843'.914 – dc20
96-32612 CIP

To the memory of M.D.W. Jeffreys

Contents

A Long Voyage

The *Surabaya*, an aging three-hundred-ton ship of the Holland Africa Line, had just left the dirty waters of the Gironde estuary, bound for the west coast of Africa, and Fintan looked at his mother as if it were for the first time. Perhaps he had never before realized how young she was, how close to him she was, like the sister he had never had. Not really beautiful, but so alive, so strong. It was late afternoon; the sun illuminated her dark gold-flecked hair, the outline of her profile, her high forehead which rounded sharply to meet her nose, the shape of her lips, her chin. There was a clear fuzz on her skin, like that of a fruit. He watched her; he loved her face.

When he turned ten, Fintan decided he would call his mother only by her nickname. Her name was Maria Luisa, but she was called Maou; Fintan, as a baby, could not pronounce her name, and so it had stuck. He had taken his mother by the hand, looked straight into her eyes, and decided: "From today on I shall call you Maou." He looked so serious that she stood speechless for a moment, then she burst out laughing, a mad laughter that occasionally took hold of her, irresistibly. Fintan had laughed, too, and that had sealed their agreement.

Maou leaned against the wooden handrail and watched the ship's wake, and Fintan watched her. It was late Sunday afternoon, 14 March 1948—a date Fintan would never forget. The sky and sea were intensely blue, almost violet. The air was still, so the ship must have been moving at the speed of the wind. A few gulls hovered in heavy flight above the rear deck, approaching, then winging away from the mast where the flag with its triple stripes fluttered like an old dish towel. From time to time they dove to the side, calling out in strange harmony with the attendant drone of the propellers.

Fintan watched his mother, and listened with almost painful attention to the sounds around him, to the gulls' cries. He felt the waves sliding under the ship's bow as they rose in a prolonged effort to lift the hull, as if taking a breath.

It was the first time. He looked at Maou's face, the left side, as it gradually became a pure profile in the brilliance of the sky and the sun. Yes, he thought, this was it, this was the first time. And still he did not understand the tightness in his throat, this feeling which made his heart beat and filled his eyes with tears, because it was also the last time. They were going away, nothing would ever be as before. Beyond the white wake the ribbon of land was fading. The silt from the estuary had suddenly given way to the deep blue of the sea. The reed-spiked fingers of sand, where the fishermen's huts looked like toys, and all the strange shapes on shore—towers, beacons, hoop nets, quarries, block-houses—all were lost to the movement of the sea, drowned in the tide.

At the prow the disc of the sun was dropping towards the horizon.

"Come and see the green flash." Maou pulled Fintan close; he thought he could feel her heartbeat through the thickness of her coat. On the first-class deck, to the fore, people were applauding, laughing about something. Bright red sailors were running amid the passengers, carrying ropes, lashing down the gangway.

Fintan realized they were not alone. There were people everywhere. They came and went, busily, continually, between the deck and their staterooms. They leaned against the railing, trying to see; they called out to each other, they took out their binoculars and telescopes. They wore gray overcoats, hats, scarves. They shoved, spoke loudly, smoked duty-free cigarettes. Fintan wanted to see Maou's profile once again, a shadow against the light of the sky. But she too was speaking, to him, her eyes shining: "Are you all right? Are you cold? Would you like to go down to the cabin; do you want to rest before dinner?"

Fintan held on to the guardrail. His eyes felt like dry, singed pebbles. He wanted to see; he did not want to forget this moment when the ship entered the deep sea, breaking away from the distant strip of land. France was being swallowed by the dark blue of the swell: fields, towns, houses, faces submerged, churned into the wake, while at the bow—beyond the silhouettes of first-class passengers poised against the railing like ruffled birds, with their shrieks and their laughter, and beyond the measured throb of the machines in the depths of the *Surabaya* which shattered on the rushing shoulders of the waves, sonorous and still in the motionless air like the fragments of a dream— while at the bow, where the sky drops into the sea, like a finger through a pupil to probe the depths of the head, the green flash exploded in sudden brilliance.

That night, their first night at sea, Fintan could not sleep. He did not move, he held his breath, to hear Maou's regular breathing, despite the vibrations and creaking of the ship's frames. His back ached with fatigue—the hours of waiting in Bordeaux, on the quay, in the cold wind; the rail journey from Marseilles. And then all the days preceding their departure, the farewells, the tears, the voice of Grandmother Aurelia telling a thousand funny stories in order not to think of what was happening. The tearing, the void left in one's memory. "Don't cry, *bellino*, suppose I come and see you there?" The slow movement of the ocean swell pressed against his chest and his head: it was a movement that took hold of you and carried you away, a movement of embrace and oblivion, like pain, like a sorrow. In the narrow bunk Fintan pressed his arms against his body, allowing the motion to roll him onto his hip. He was falling, perhaps, like before, during the war; he was sliding backwards, towards the other side of the world. "What is there out there? Out there?" He could hear Aunt Rosa's voice: "What's so wonderful about that place? Don't you die out there?" He wanted to see beyond the green flash, beyond the point where the sky dropped to the sea. "Once upon a time there was a country where you arrived after a long voyage, a country where you arrived when everything had been forgotten, when you no longer even knew, who you were. . . ."

Grandmother Aurelia's voice resounded upon the sea. In the hard hollow of his bunk, with the engines vibrating through his body, Fintan listened to the voice talking to itself, trying to hold the thread of the other life. Already it pained him to forget. "I hate him, I hate him. I don't want to leave, I don't want to go there I hate him, he's not my father!" The frames of the ship groaned with each wave. Fintan tried to hear his mother's quiet breathing. He whispered loudly, "Maou! Maou!" When she did not reply, he slid out of his bunk. The cabin was lit by a vent above the door, six vertical slits. There was an electric bulb just on the other side, in the corridor. As he was moving he could see the filament shining through each slit. It was an inner stateroom, without a porthole; it was all they could afford. The air was gray, stifling, and damp. His eyes wide open, Fintan tried to make out his mother's sleeping shape on the other berth as she too was transported backwards across the moving ocean. The frames of the ship creaked, laboring across the swell as it pushed, restrained, then pushed again.

Fintan's eyes filled with tears; he did not really know why. He felt a pain deep within his body, at a point where his memory was unravelling and disappearing.

"I don't want to go to Africa." That was something he had never said to Maou, or to Grandmother Aurelia, or to anyone. On the contrary, he had wanted to, very much; it had burned within him, made him sleepless, in Marseilles, in Grandmother Aurelia's little apartment. It had burned within him and filled him with fever, in the train heading for Bordeaux. He did not want to hear any more voices or see any more faces. He had to close his eyes and block his ears to make it all easy. He wanted to be someone else who would be strong, who would not speak, would not cry, would not feel his heart pounding or his stomach aching.

The man would speak English, he would have two vertical wrinkles between his eyebrows, the way men do, and Maou would no longer be his mother. The man waiting, there, at the end of the journey, would *never* be his father. He was a stranger who had written letters so that they would join him in Africa. He was a man with neither wife nor child, a man they did not know, whom they had never seen — so why was he waiting? He had a name, a fine name, that was true; his name was Geoffroy Allen. But when they arrived, at the other end of the journey, they would pass by very quickly, there on the quay, and the man would see nothing, recognize no one, and would just have to go home empty-handed.

Up on deck the wind had begun to blow in the night: ocean wind, whistling under doors, slapping faces. Fintan walked against the wind towards the bow. The tears in his eyes were salty like the spray. They flowed freely now, because of the wind which tore at the land. Life in Marseilles, in Grandmother Aurelia's apartment; and before that, life in Saint-Martin, the long walk to the other side of the mountains, to the valley of the Stura, to Santa Anna. The wind blew and carried him away and called forth his tears. Fintan walked on deck, along the long metal wall, and was blinded by the electric bulbs and the black void of the sea and the sky. He did not feel the cold. Barefoot, he moved forward, holding on to the handrail, towards the deserted first-class deck. As he went by the cabins he could see silhouettes through the windows, through the muslin curtains; he could hear women's voices, laughter, music. At the end of the deck was the main first-class lounge, where people still sat at tables, in red armchairs; the men were smoking and playing cards. Further forward was the cargo deck, its hatches all closed, then the mast, the fo'c'sle lit by a yellow lamp, then the violent wind and the waves breaking in a cloud of vapor which shone on the puddles like gusts of rain on a road. Fintan wedged his back against the wall, between the windows of the lounge, and he watched, motionless, almost breathless. He stood there watching for such a long time that he felt he was falling forward, that the ship was plummeting towards the depths of the ocean. The black void of ocean and sky rose in his eyes. A Dutch sailor, Christof, happened to be walking along the deck and found Fintan just as he was about to faint. He was carried into the lounge, and after he was questioned by the first mate, Fintan was taken back to Maou's cabin.

Maou had never known such happiness. The *Surabaya* was a pleasant ship, with covered decks where you could take a stroll or stretch out in a deck chair to read and dream. You could come and go as you pleased. Mr. Heylings, the first mate, was a tall, strong man, somewhat red in the face, almost bald; and he spoke French fluently. After Fintan's nocturnal adventure he befriended the boy. He took him, and Maou as well, to visit the engine room. He was very proud of the *Surabaya*'s engines, old bronze turbines which turned slowly, "with a clocklike sound," he said. He explained the workings of the cogs and the connecting rods. Fintan stood for a long time in admiration before the valves which rose in turn and, on the other side of the openwork deck, the twin axles of the propellers.

The *Surabaya* had been at sea for days. One evening Mr. Heylings took Maou and Fintan up onto the bridge. A string of dark islands hung from the horizon. "Look, Madeira, Funchal." Magical names; the ship would draw nearer during the night.

When the sun touched the sea, everyone, except for a few skeptics, would rush to the foredeck next to first class to watch out for the green flash. But every evening it was the same: at the last moment, the sun melted into the haze which rose from the horizon to eclipse the miracle.

It was the evenings Maou liked best. As the ship approached the coast of Africa, there was a gentle listlessness in the air at dusk, a warm breath caressing the deck and smoothing the sea. Seated side by side in their deck chairs, Maou and Fintan spoke quietly to each other. It was the time for strolls along the deck; passengers went back and forth, greeted one another. The Botrous, with whom they shared a table at mealtimes, had a business in Dakar. Mrs. O'Gilby was the wife of an English officer stationed at Accra. A young French nurse called Geneviève was accompanied by an Italian man with lacquered hair, her *chevalier servant*. A nun from the Ticino, Maria, was headed for the heart of Africa, Niger; she had a very smooth face with large, sea green eyes and a childlike smile. Maou had never known people like this; she had never imagined that she might one day be with them, to share their adventure. She spoke to everyone, eagerly; she took tea, went into first class after dinner, sat at the tables—so white, the silverware gleaming and the wineglasses shivering to the rhythm of the bronze valves.

Fintan listened to the melody of Maou's voice. He liked her Italian accent, its music. He fell asleep on his chair. Tall Mr. Heylings picked him up and carried him back to his narrow berth. When Fintan opened his eyes, he saw the six vents above the cabin door, shining mysteriously as on their first night at sea.

Yet he did not sleep. Eyes open in the half-light, he waited for Maou to return. The ship pitched heavily, frames creaking. It was then that Fintan could call up his memories. Things of the past had not disappeared, they were merely hidden in shadow—if you were watchful, and listened carefully, they would be there. The fields of grass in the valley of the Stura, the summer sounds; the trips to the river; the children's voices, crying Gianni! Sandro! Sonia! Drops of cool water on skin, light catching Esther's hair. In Saint-Martin, even further back in time, the sound of the water rushing down, the brook cascading down the main street. It was all coming back, penetrating the narrow cabin, crowding the gray, heavy air. Then the ship carried it all away again on the waves, sweeping everything in its wake. The vibration of the engines was stronger than memories; they became feeble and mute.

There was laughter in the corridor; Maou's clear tones and the deep, slow voice of the Dutchman. They were saying, "Shsh. . . ." The door opened. Fintan squeezed his eyelids shut. He could smell Maou's perfume; he could hear the rustling of cloth as she undressed in the darkness. It was wonderful to be with her, so near her, day and night. He could smell her skin, her hair. Long ago, in the room, in Italy . . . nighttime, windows sealed with blue paper, the drone of the American planes on their way to bomb Genoa. He would snuggle close to Maou in the bed, hiding his head in her hair. He could hear her breathing, the sound of her heart. When she fell asleep, there was something soft, light, a breeze, a breath; what he had been waiting for.

He remembered the time he had seen her naked. It was summer, in Santa Anna. The Germans were very near — you could hear the thunder of the guns in the valley. In the room the shutters were closed. It was hot. Fintan had opened the door without making a sound. Maou lay on the bed, naked on the sheet. Her body seemed immense, all white, thin, you could see her ribs, the black tufts of her armpits, the dark buttons of her breasts, the triangle of pubic hair. There had been the same gray air as now in the cabin; the same closeness. Fintan had stood by the half-opened door and watched. He remembered the burning sensation on his face, as if that white body were glowing with heat. Then he had taken two steps backwards, holding his breath. In the kitchen flies were divebombing against the windows. And a column of ants in the sink; the copper tap dripping. Why did he remember these things?

The *Surabaya* was a large steel box taking away his memories, devouring them. The noise of the engines did not stop. Fintan pictured the connecting rods and the axles shining in the bowels of the ship, the twin screws turning in opposite directions, churning the waves. Everything was being swept away. They might be going to the other end of the world. They were going to Africa. The names which he had always heard—Maou pronounced them slowly—familiar and frightening names: Onitsha, Niger. Onitsha. So far away, the other end of the world. The man who was waiting: Geoffroy Allen. Maou had shown Fintan the letters. She read them as if she were reciting a prayer, a lesson. She would stop, she would look at Fintan, her eyes shining with impatience. When you're in Onitsha. I'm waiting for you both, I love you. She said, "Your father wrote, your father says . . ." This man, with the same name. I am waiting for you. So every turn of the propeller in the black water of the ocean meant the same, repeating these names, frightening and familiar, Geoffroy Allen, Onitsha, Niger: tender and threatening words, I'm waiting for you, in Onitsha, on the banks of the river Niger. I am your father.

The sun, the sea. The *Surabaya* seemed motionless on the vast flat expanse, motionless like a castle of steel against the near whiteness of a sky emptied of birds, while the sun slid towards the horizon.

Motionless like the sky. Day after day, only this hard sea, the air moving at the speed of the ship, the slow path of the sun across the steel walls, its glare bearing down upon forehead and chest, burning deep inside.

Fintan could not sleep at night. He sat up on deck, at the spot where he had nearly fainted the first evening, and watched the sky for shooting stars.

Monsieur Botrou had spoken of showers of stars. But as the sky swung slowly before the ship's mast, not a single star set off on its own.

Maou came to sit next to Fintan. She sat right on the deck, her back against the wall of the lounge, her blue skirt pulled over her knees, her bare arms encircling her legs. She didn't speak; like him, she was watching the night. Perhaps she did not see the same things. In the lounge, passengers were smoking, speaking loudly. The English officers were playing darts.

Fintan looked at Maou's profile, as he had done on the day of their departure while the ship floated down the estuary. She was so young. She had worked her lovely chestnut hair into one long plait and wrapped it around the back of her head. He loved the way she poked the long, shiny, black pins into her hair. The ocean sun had browned her face, her arms, her legs. One evening, as Maou came near, Monsieur Botrou had called out, "Here comes the African woman!" Fintan had felt his heart beat faster, inexplicably, with pleasure.

One morning Mr. Heylings called him up again onto the poop deck to show him other black shapes on the horizon. He said magical words: "Tenerife, Gran Canaria, Lanzarote." Through the binoculars Fintan could see the trembling mountains, the cone of the volcano, clouds fluttering from the peaks, dark green valleys above the sea, the smoke of ships hidden by the crests of waves. All day long the islands lay there, to port, like a pod of petrified whales. Birds had even appeared at the stern, squawking seagulls circling above the deck to eye the people below, who watched in turn as they tossed bread for the gulls to catch; then they flew off again, and the islands were nothing more than faint dots, barely visible on the horizon.

It was so hot in the windowless cabin that Fintan could not stay in his berth. He went to sit with Maou on the deck. They watched the stars swaying above them. When he felt the drowsiness rising in him he laid his head on Maou's shoulder. At dawn he awoke in the cabin. The coolness of morning came in through the door. The electric bulb still shone in the corridor. Christof would turn the lights off as soon as he got up.

The vibrations of the engines seemed closer: toiling, a steady puffing. The two oiled shafts turned in opposite directions in the heart of the *Surabaya*. Beneath his naked body Fintan could feel the damp sheet. He dreamt he had wet his bed and the fright woke him up, only to find that his entire body was covered with tiny, transparent spots, which he tore open with his nails. It was terrible. Fintan sobbed with pain and fright. Roused by Maou, Dr. Lang leaned over the berth, looked at Fintan's body without touching him and then said, simply, in his curious Alsatian accent, "It's scabies, my dear woman." In the ship's medicine chest he found a bottle of talcum powder, and Maou sprinkled it over the spots, smoothing them gently with her hand. At the end they were both laughing. That was all. Maou exclaimed, "A barnyard disease!"

The days were so long. Perhaps it was the summertime light, or the horizon, so far away, with nothing to hold one's gaze. It was like waiting, hour after hour, until you no longer knew what you were waiting for. Maou stayed in the dining room after breakfast, next to the greasy window, which blurred the color of the sea. She was writing. With the white paper spread flat on the mahogany table and the inkwell wedged in the hollow space provided for a glass, she was writing, her head somewhat inclined. She had got into the habit of lighting up a cigarette, a Player's bought in packets of one hundred at the steward's shop; she let the cigarette burn by itself on the edge of the ashtray engraved with the initials of the Holland Africa Line. Was she writing stories, or letters — she wasn't really sure. Words. She began, not knowing which direction she would take — French, Italian, sometimes even English, it made no difference. She simply liked to do it, to dream while watching the sea, the soft smoke swirling; to write with the slow rocking of the ship as it moved on, hour after hour, day after day, towards the unknown. Later, the heat of the sun burned the deck, and she had to leave the dining room. To write, listening to the rustling of water against the hull, as if one were travelling up an endless river.

San Remo, she wrote, *the square in the shade of the tall trees in full bloom, the fountain, the clouds above the sea, the scarabs in the warm air.*

I feel the breeze on my eyes.

In my hands I hold the prey of silence.

I wait for the quiver of pleasure from your gaze on my body.

I dreamt last night that I saw you at the foot of the lane of charms, in Fiesole. You were like a blind man searching for his home. Outside I could hear voices murmuring insults, or prayers.

I remember, you spoke to me of the death of children, of war. The years they have not lived gouge gaping holes in the walls of our houses.

She wrote: *Geoffroy, you are in me, I am in you. The time which kept us apart no longer exists. Time had effaced me. In traces on the sea, in whitecap signs, I read your memory. I cannot lose what I see, I cannot forget what I am. It is for you that I make this voyage.*

She dreamt as the cigarette burned away, as the sheet of paper filled with words. Her letters became entangled, and there were large, white gaps between them. Aurelia used to say she had a slanting, affected handwriting, the tall letters struck with a long curving train, the ts crossed diagonally.

I remember the last time we spoke, in San Remo; you spoke to me of the silence of the desert, as if you were going to go back against the flow of time, as far as Meroë, to find the truth; and now I myself, here in the silence and the wilderness of the sea, feel I am going back in time to find the truth of my life, there, in Onitsha.

To write was to dream. Out there, once they reached Onitsha, everything would be different, everything would be easy. There would be the great plains of grass that Geoffroy had described, the trees so tall, and the river so wide you might think it was the sea, the horizon lost in mirages of water and sky. There would be gentle hills, planted with mango trees, and red earthen houses with their roofs of woven leaves. Up above the river, surrounded by trees, would be the large wooden house with its tin roof painted white, with its terrace and the thick growth of bamboo. And the strange name, Ibusun; Geoffroy had explained its meaning in the language of the river people: the place where one sleeps.

That is where they would live, all of Geoffroy's family. It would be their home and their homeland. When she had told her friend Léone in Marseilles—it was like telling a secret—she had been astonished by Léone's reply, her high-pitched condescension: "And that is where you are going to live, you poor thing? In such a hut?" Maou wanted to speak of the grass, so tall you could disappear in it altogether, the river so vast and slow, the steamships of the United Africa. Speak of the forest dark as night, inhabited by thousands of birds. But she had preferred to say nothing. She had simply said yes, in that house. Above all she had not dared say the name of Ibusun, for Léone would have given her a tongue-lashing, and that would have vexed her. Or even worse yet, Léone might have burst out laughing.

Now it was good to wait, in the ship's dining room, with these words she was writing. Every minute brought them closer to Onitsha, closer to Ibusun. Fintan sat across from her with his elbows on the table, watching her. His stare was black and piercing, softened by his long eyelashes which curled like a girl's, and his fine, smooth hair, chestnut like Maou's.

From the time he was very young she had repeated the names to him, nearly every day, the names of the river and its islands, the forest, the plains of grass, the trees. He already knew everything about mangos and yams, before having tasted either. He knew the slow movement of the steamboats going up the river to Onitsha to deliver goods to the wharf before they left again, laden with oil and plantains.

Fintan watched Maou. He said, "Speak to me in Italian, Maou."

"What would you like me to say?"

"Poems."

She recited verses by Manzoni, Alfieri, *Antigone*, *Mary Stuart*, lines she had learned by heart, at the high school San Pier d'Arena in Genoa:

> Incender lascia,
> tu che perir non dei, da me quel rogo,
> che coll'amato mio fratel mi accolga.

Fummo in duo corpi un'alma sola in vita,
sola una fiamma anco le morte nostre
spoglie consumi, e in una polve unisca.

Fintan listened to the music of the words; it always made him feel like crying. Outside, the sun glistened on the sea. The warm wind of the Sahara blew against the waves, red dust rained upon the deck, on the portholes. Fintan would have liked the journey to last forever.

One morning, shortly before noon, the coast of Africa hove into sight. It was Mr. Heylings who came to fetch Maou and Fintan: he led them up onto the bridge, next to the helmsman. The passengers were getting ready for lunch. Maou and Fintan had lost their appetite; they had come up barefoot, not to waste any time. On the horizon, to port, Africa was a long gray strip, very flat, hardly above sea level, and yet extraordinarily sharp and visible. They hadn't seen land for such a long time. Fintan thought it looked like the Gironde estuary.

And yet he did not tire of looking at this vision of Africa, even when Maou left to join the Botrous in the dining room. Strange and faraway, it seemed the sort of place one would never reach.

From then on, every moment, Fintan would watch the line of land; it occupied him from dawn to dusk, and even into the night. The land slipped by, very slowly, yet remained the same, gray and precise against the brilliance of the sea and the sky. From that land came the warm breeze tossing sand against the windows of the ship. The land had changed the sea: now the waves rushed towards it to die against the beaches. The waters were confused, greenish, mixed with rain, sluggish. You could see large birds. They flew near the bow of the *Surabaya*, tilting their heads to look at mankind. Mr. Heylings knew their names, they were gannets, frigate birds. One evening there was even a clumsy pelican which got caught in the rigging of the derricks.

At dawn, before anyone else was up, Fintan was already on deck to look at Africa. Tiny birds flew overhead, shining like pewter, scooping the air with piercing cries, cries from land that caused Fintan's heart to beat with something like impatience, as if the day about to begin would be full of marvels, the prelude to a fairy tale.

The morning brought schools of dolphins, and flying fish bursting out of the waves in the path of the bow. Like the sand, insects arrived on board: flies, dragonflies, even a praying mantis, which stuck to the dining room windowsill; Christof delighted in making it pray.

The sun beat down on the ribbon of land. The evening breeze raised great, gray clouds veiling the sky, washing the twilight with yellow. It was so hot in the cabin that Maou fell asleep naked, wrapped in the white sheet, which revealed, by its transparency, her dark body. Mosquitoes made their appearance, as did the bitter taste of quinine. Every night Maou anointed Fintan's back and legs with calamine lotion. Names went the rounds of the dinner tables: Saint-Louis, Dakar. There were other names Fintan loved to hear: Langue de Barbarie and Gorée, names soft and terrible at the same time. Monsieur Botrou told them that it was in Gorée that the slaves had been locked away in the old days, before they were to leave for America or the West Indies. Africa resounded with names; Fintan recited them quietly, a litany, as if in saying them he could seize their secret, the very reason for the motion of the ship carving its wake through the sea.

Then, one day, at the end of the interminable gray strip there was land, real red and ochre land, with foaming reefs, islands, and the immense, pale stain of a river meeting the sea. That morning Christof was burned while adjusting the pipes of the hot water supply for the showers. In the empty dawn his cry roared down the corridor. Fintan jumped out of his berth. There was noise, confusion, the sound of running at the end of the corridor. Maou called Fintan back and closed the door behind them. But Christof's cries of pain drowned the creaking and vibrating of the engines.

Shortly before noon the *Surabaya* made landfall at Dakar, and Christof was the first ashore, to be taken to hospital. He had been burned on half of his body.

As Fintan walked along the waterfront with Maou he shivered with every seagull's cry. There was a strong, pungent smell; it made you cough. So that was what was hidden in the name Dakar. The smell of peanuts and oil, the acrid, thin smoke floating everywhere, on the wind, in one's hair and clothes. As far as the sun.

Fintan breathed in the odor. It entered him, soaked into his body. Odor of this dusty earth, odor of the very blue sky, the gleaming palm trees, the white houses. Odor of women and children dressed in rags. Odor which possessed the town. Fintan had always been there; Africa was already a memory.

20

Maou hated the town from the first instant. "Look, Fintan, look at these people! Policemen everywhere!" She pointed to the civil servants in their stiff uniforms, with their helmets that made them look like real policemen. They wore waistcoats and gold pocket watches in the style of the last century. There were also poorly shaven European tradesmen in short trousers, cigarette butts dangling from their lips. Senegalese policemen stood solidly, observing the line of dockers trickling with sweat. "And the smell, these peanuts, it gets into your throat, you can't breathe." They had to get away from the waterfront. Maou took Fintan's hand and led him towards the gardens, followed by a crowd of begging children. She looked questioningly at Fintan. Did he also hate this town? But it was all so strong—the smell, the light, the shining faces, the shouting children—a whirling, a chiming, with no room for feelings.

The *Surabaya* was a refuge, an island. The cabin was a hiding place of gray, sweltering heat and shadow, with the sound of water from the shower room at the end of the corridor. There was no window. Africa, after so many days at sea, made one's heart beat too quickly.

On the piers of Dakar there were only barrels of oil and that smell reaching to the heart of the sky. Maou said it made her want to vomit. "Oh, why does it smell so strong?" Goods were being unloaded, to the creaking of the derrick and the shouts of the dockers. When she had to go out, Maou sheltered beneath her blue parasol. The sun poured its heat onto houses and dusty streets. Monsieur and Madame Botrou had to take the train to Saint-Louis. Dakar resounded with the noise of lorries and cars, children's voices, radios. The sky was filled with shouts. And the smell, never ending, like an invisible cloud. Even sheets, clothes, and the palms of one's hands were saturated with it. A yellow sky closed over the huge city with its weight of late-afternoon heat. And suddenly, like a fountain, thin, sharp, the voice of the muezzin calling to prayer above the tin roofs.

Maou had had enough of the ship. She decided to go with the Botrous to Saint-Louis. In her hotel room, while she thought Fintan was outside playing in the garden, she began to wash. She stood quite naked in a tub of cold water in the middle of the blood red tiles and squeezed a sponge over her head. The shutters of the high windows let in a gray daylight like that of the room, long ago, in Santa Anna. Fintan crept in, silently, and stood watching Maou. It was a vision both beautiful and tormenting—her thin, pale body, with its ribs visible, her shoulders and legs so brown, her breasts with their plum-colored nipples, and the sound of the water trickling down her woman's body in the half-light of the room, a sound of soft rain, while her hands raised the sponge to squeeze it over her hair. Fintan stood motionless. The smell of the oil was everywhere, even here, in this room, seeping into Maou's body and hair, perhaps forever.

So this, then, was Africa, this warm and violent city, the yellow sky beating with a secret pulse of light. The Botrous invited Maou and Fintan to Gorée to visit the fort before returning to Dakar. In the bay the launch glided towards the dark line of the island. The accursed fortress where the slaves awaited their journey to hell: through the middle of the cells ran a gutter to drain off the urine. On the walls were rings where the chains had been attached. This was Africa, this darkness heavy with suffering, this odor of sweat from the depths of jails, this odor of death. Maou felt disgusted and ashamed. She did not want to stay in Gorée, she wanted to go back to Dakar as quickly as possible.

That evening Fintan was hot with fever. Maou's hands passed over his face, fresh and light. "Drink your quinine, bellino, drink." The sun beat down, even now, even at night, right into the windowless cabin. "I want to see Grandmother Aurelia again—when are we going back to France?" Fintan wandered in and out of delirium. The acrid smell of peanuts and the shadow of Gorée lingered in the cabin. There was a hum now, the hum of Africa. Insects marched around the lamps. "What about Christof? Is he going to die?"

The sound of the engines had started up again, with the slow roll of the swell, the creaking of the frames each time the bow topped a wave. Nighttime, and they were travelling towards other ports: Freetown, Monrovia, Takoradi, Cotonou. With the motion of the ship Maou felt that the fever was receding, slipping away. Fintan lay motionless on his berth, listening to Maou's breathing and the breathing of the sea. The burning he felt at the back of his eyes and in the depths of his body was the sun, suspended above the island of Gorée in the middle of the yellow sky, the accursed sun of slaves chained to their cells, flogged by the foremen of the peanut plantations. They were slipping away, beyond the twilight.

At dawn there was a strange, disquieting sound on the *Surabaya*'s foredeck. Fintan got up to listen. Through the half open door of the cabin, along the corridor still lit by electric lamps, came the noise — dull, monotonous, and regular. A faraway tapping noise on the ship's hull. If you put your hand on the wall in the corridor, you could feel the vibrations. Fintan dressed hurriedly and ran off barefoot to trace the sound.

Many people had gathered on deck, Englishmen dressed in white linen, ladies wearing hats and veils. The sun beat down on the sea. Fintan walked along the first-class deck towards the fo'c'sle, where you could see the hatches. Suddenly, as if looking down from the balcony of a building, Fintan discovered the source of the sound: the entire foredeck of the *Surabaya* was crowded with blacks. They crouched down and were beating with hammers on the hatches, the hull, and the frames to remove the rust.

Above the coast of Africa, above the horizon rose the sun, ringed with what seemed a halo of sand. Already the warm air was smoothing the sea. The blacks clung to the deck and the frames of the ship as if to the body of a giant animal and pounded to an irregular beat with their small, sharp hammers. The noise reverberated throughout the entire ship, ever louder against sea and sky, as if penetrating the strip of land on the horizon like a hard, heavy music, one which filled the heart, unforgettable.

Maou joined Fintan on the deck. "Why are they doing that?" Fintan asked. "Poor souls," said Maou. She explained that the blacks' job was to remove the rust from the ship in order to pay for their own and their families' transportation to the next port. The banging obeyed an incomprehensible, chaotic rhythm, as if it were they now who were causing the *Surabaya* to move on through the sea.

They were headed for Takoradi, Lomé, Cotonou; they were headed for Conakry, Sherbro, Lavannah, Edina, Manna, Sinou, Accra, Bonny, Calabar. . . . Maou and Fintan stayed for hours on deck, watching the endless coast: the dark land on the horizon, opening to unknown estuaries, so vast, carrying fresh river water to the center of the sea along with tree trunks and rafts of grass twisted like snakes, and embryonic islands fringed with foam. Then heavy birds filled the sky above the stern, cocking their heads, their keen gaze sweeping over the ship and its foreign passengers who dared linger upon the boundaries of their territory.

On the foredeck the blacks continued their hammering. The light was dazzling. The men streamed with sweat. At four o'clock, at the sound of a bell, they stopped work. The Dutch sailors went down onto the cargo deck to collect the small hammers and distribute food. There were tarpaulins on the deck, makeshift shelter. Although it was not allowed, the women lit campfires. They were Peulhs, Wolofs, Mandingos, identifiable by their long, white robes, their blue tunics, or their pearl-studded trousers. They sat down round a tin teapot with a long curved spout. Now that the sound of the hammering had stopped, Fintan could hear the babble of voices, the laughter of children. The wind brought the smell of food and cigarette smoke. On the first-class promenade deck the English officers, the colonial administrators in their light-colored clothing, and the ladies with their hats and veils looked distractedly upon the crowd pressing on the cargo deck with their multicolored washing floating in the sun. They were talking of other things, their thoughts were elsewhere. Even Maou, after the first day or two, no longer heard the noise of the hammering on the ship's frames. But each morning when it began Fintan gave a start. He could not tear his gaze away from the blacks living on the cargo deck to the fore of the ship. At first light he would run barefoot to the barrier, propping his feet against the wall to have a better view over the railing. With the first banging sound he felt his heart beat faster, as if it were music. The men lifted their hammers one after the other and brought them down: without a cry, without a song, and other blows replied from the other end of the ship, and still others, and soon the entire hull vibrated, pulsated like a living animal.

And the sea so heavy, the estuaries of mud clouding the deep blue, and the coast of Africa, at times so near you could make out the white houses among the trees and hear the breakers rumbling against the reefs. Mr. Heylings showed Maou and Fintan the Gambia River, the islands of Formosa, the coast of Sierra Leone where so many ships had been wrecked. He pointed out the coast of the Krus and said, "At Manna, at la Grande Bassa, and at the Cape of Palms there are no lights, so the Krus make fires on the beach as if it were the entry to Monrovia harbor or the lighthouse on the Sierra Leone peninsula, and the ships go up onto the coast. They pillage the ships they wreck."

Untiringly, Fintan watched the squatting men who beat against the hull with their hammers; it was music, a secret language, as if they were telling the tale of those who were shipwrecked along the coast of the Krus. One evening, without telling Maou, he jumped over the railing and climbed down the ladder to the cargo deck. He slipped between the containers until he reached the big hatches where the blacks were camped. It was twilight, the ship moved slowly across the muddy sea towards one of the major ports: Conakry, Freetown, perhaps Monrovia. The deck still radiated the heat of the sun. There was the smell of grease, oil, the acid smell of sweat. Sheltered against the rusty frames, women rocked their little children. Naked boys played with bottles and empty cans. There was a tiredness. The men lay on bits of cloth, sleeping, or watching the sky, silently. It was very gentle, very slow; the sea trawled long waves from the depths of the ocean and the waves slid under the ship's keel, indifferent, to the hub of the earth.

No one spoke. The only sound was that of a voice on the foredeck singing, alone and muted, to the slow lift of the waves and the breathing of the engines. One voice, no more than "ah" or "eya-oh," not quite sad, not quite a lament, the soft voice of a man sitting against a container, clothed in stained rags, his face ridged with deep scars on his forehead and cheeks.

The prow of the *Surabaya* lifted on the swell, tossing an occasional burst of spray, rainbow-clear, above the deck, a cold cloud on the burning men. Fintan sat down on the deck to listen to the song of the man in rags. Children approached, shyly. No one spoke. The sky turned yellow; then night fell, and the man continued to sing.

After some time a Dutch sailor spotted Fintan and came to get him. Mr. Heylings was not pleased. "You're not allowed on the cargo deck and you know it!" Maou was in tears; she had been dreadfully frightened, that a wave had carried him off, had drowned him; she had watched the wake, as it continued its cruel path—she had wanted to stop the ship! She held Fintan against her, she could say no more. It was the first time he had ever seen her cry, and he cried too. "I won't do it again, Maou, I won't go back on deck."

Later he asked, "Tell me, Maou, why did you marry an Englishman?" He said it so seriously that she burst out laughing. She hugged him so tight that his feet lifted off the ground, and while she held him she spun around as if she were dancing, waltzing. He must never forget that moment, ever. The twilight at the bow of the ship; the slow song of the man in rags, and Maou, holding Fintan in her arms and dancing on the deck, to dizziness.

They were heading for other ports, other river mouths. Manna, Setta Krus, Tabu, Sassandra, invisible among the dark palm trees; and islands, appearing, disappearing, rivers rolling their silt-laden waters, pushing errant tree trunks towards the sea like masts torn off in a shipwreck; Bandama, Comoe, lagoons, immense sandy beaches. On the first-class deck Maou was speaking with an English officer whose name was Gerald Simpson.

By chance he too was going to Onitsha. He had been appointed D.O., District Officer; he was about to take up his new post. "I've heard of your husband," he said to Maou, nothing more. He was a tall, thin man with a hooked nose, a handlebar moustache, small, steel-rimmed glasses, close-cropped blond hair. He spoke softly, almost whispering, and did not move his narrow lips, which suggested disdain. He pronounced the name of each port, each cape, as he glanced at the faraway coast. He spoke of the Krus, turning his shoulders slightly towards the bow, the light shining on the circle of his glasses. Fintan took an instant dislike to him.

"These . . . people, they move about continuously, going from town to town, quite capable of selling anything."

He gestured vaguely towards the man who sang in the evening following the rhythm of the waves.

There was another man who spoke with Maou, an Englishman, or perhaps he was Belgian, with a strange name—he was called Florizel. Very tall and fat, with a very red face which was constantly bathed in sweat; he drank one brown beer after another and spoke loudly in a strange accent. When Maou and Fintan were there, he would tell terrible stories about Africa, stories of children kidnapped and sold on the marketplace cut up in little pieces, stories of ropes stretched taut across the road at night to trip up cyclists, who were then also turned into meat pies; then the one about a parcel addressed to a rich businessman in Abidjan which, when it was opened at customs, was found to contain the hacked-up pieces, wrapped in brown paper, of the body of a little girl, hands and feet and head. He told it all in his loud voice and chuckled to himself noisily. Maou took Fintan by the arm and pulled him away, an angry quiver in her voice. "He's a liar, don't believe what he tells you." Florizel travelled all over Africa selling Swiss watches. He said, pompously, "Africa is a grand lady, she has given me everything." He looked on the English officers with scorn, so pale and stilted in their uniforms of cartoon conquerors.

They were heading for the lagoons, the Cape of Palms, Cavally, Grand Bassam, Trois Pointes. Clouds lifted away from the dark earth, laden with sand and insects. One morning Mr. Heylings brought Fintan a large sheet of paper: a stick insect sat there, immobile and fabulous.

At dawn the *Surabaya* pulled into the bay of Takoradi.

The cart moved along the road directly to the sea. Maou sat very straight, sheltering under her straw hat, wearing a voile dress and white tennis shoes. Fintan admired her tanned profile, her shining bronzed legs. At the front of the rickety cart the driver held the reins of a broken-winded horse. He looked back from time to time at Maou and Fintan. He was a black giant of a man, a Ghan with a magnificent name—he was called Yao. The Englishman Simpson had insisted on discussing the price of the trip in pidgin. "You know, with these people . . ." Maou didn't want him to go with them. She wanted to be alone with Fintan. It was the first time they were going into Africa.

The cart moved slowly along the straight line of road, stirring up behind it a cloud of red dust. On either side were immense plantations of coconut palms and huts brimming with children.

Then the sound: Fintan heard it first, through the clip-clop of the horse's hooves and the creaking metal of the cart. A powerful, sweet sound, like wind in the trees.

"Can you hear it? It's the sea."

Maou tried to see through the trunks of the coconut palms. Then suddenly they were there. The beach opened out before them, brilliantly white, long rollers tumbling over one another in a carpet of foam.

Yao stopped the cart in the shelter of the coconut palms and hitched the horse. Already Fintan was running on the beach, leading Maou by the hand. The hot wind surrounded them, tossed the hem of Maou's loose dress, threatened her hat. She laughed, peals of laughter.

Together they ran to the sea, not even removing their shoes, until the frothy water rose around their legs. In a moment they were soaked from head to foot. Fintan went back to take off his clothes. He placed a branch on them to keep them from blowing away. Maou remained clothed. She took off only her tennis shoes and threw them back onto the dry sand. Waves came in from the high seas, sliding in with a rumble, rippling on the sand, tossing their sparkling water which then withdrew, sucking at their legs. Maou called, "Be careful! Give me your hand!" Together they fell into the next wave. Maou's white dress clung to her body. She held her straw hat as if she had fished it from the water. She had never known such intoxication, such freedom.

The beach was vast and empty to the west, marked by the line of coconut palms that led to the cape. On the other side were the fishermen's pirogues, beached on the sand like tree trunks thrown up in a storm. Children ran along the beach in the distance, their cries penetrating the sound of the sea.

In the shade of the coconut palms, next to the cart, Yao waited, smoking. When Maou sat down on the sand to dry her dress and her hat, he came over to her. His face expressed a certain disapproval: he pointed to the spot where Fintan and Maou had been swimming and said, in pidgin, "Last year, an Englishwoman died here. She drowned."

Maou explained to Fintan. She looked frightened. Fintan looked at the sea, so beautiful, glistening, the bevelled waves gliding across the mirror of sand. How could anyone die here? That is what her expression meant to say; that's what Maou was thinking.

They tried to stay longer on the beach. Tall Yao went back to the shade of the coconut trees to sit and smoke. There was no other sound, only the waves wearing away at the reefs, the swish of water on the sand. The burning wind shook the palms. The sky was a blue so intense, so cruel, it made one dizzy.

Once there was a flight of birds across the waves, close to the foam. "Look!" cried Maou. "Pelicans." There was something terrible and mortal now on this beach. When it dried, Maou's hat looked like a piece of flotsam.

She stood up. The salt water had stiffened her dress, the sun was scalding their faces. Fintan got dressed. They were thirsty. Yao cracked a coconut on a sharp pointed rock. Maou was the first to drink. She wiped her mouth with her hand then passed the nut to Fintan. The milk was acid. Yao then skinned the milk-soaked flesh. He sucked on the pieces. In the shade his face shone like black metal.

Maou said, "We have to get back to the ship now." She was shivering in the hot wind.

When they got back to the *Surabaya*, Maou was burning with fever. At nightfall she was shivering in her berth. The ship's doctor was not on board.

"What's the matter with me, Fintan? I'm so cold, I've got no strength left."

There was a taste of quinine in her mouth. She got up several times during the night to try to throw up. Fintan sat by her berth, holding her hand. "You'll be all right, you'll see, it's nothing." He looked at her in the gray light of the corridor. He listened to the creaking of the fenders against the dock, the rubbing groan of the mooring lines. In the cabin it was hot and close and there were mosquitoes. Outside on deck was the glow of electric storms, clouds tumbling against each other in silence. Maou finally fell asleep, but Fintan wasn't sleepy. He felt the fatigue, the loneliness. The sun beat on into the night, on his face, on his shoulders. As he leaned against the railing he tried to make out, somewhere beyond the jetty, the dark line where the waves broke.

"When will we be there?" Maou didn't know. Yesterday, the day before, she had asked Mr. Heylings. He had spoken of days, weeks. There were goods to be unloaded, other ports, more days spent waiting. Fintan was aware of a growing impatience. He wanted to arrive, there, at that port, at the end of the journey, at the end of the coast of Africa. He wanted to stop, to penetrate the dark line of the coast, cross rivers and forests, to Onitsha. It was a magical name. A magnetic name. There was no resisting it.

"When we get to Onitsha . . ." That's what Maou used to say. It was a very beautiful, very mysterious name, like a forest, like the meandering of a river. Grandmother Aurelia, in her room in Marseilles, had a painting above her huge, humped bed of a clearing in a forest where a herd of stags was resting. Each time Maou spoke of Onitsha, Fintan thought it must be like that, like the clearing, with the green light piercing the foliage of the tall trees.

"Will he be there, when the ship arrives?"

Fintan could not speak about Geoffroy in any other way. He could not say the word *father*. Maou sometimes said *Geoffroy*, and sometimes she called him by his surname, Allen. It had been so long; perhaps she no longer knew him.

Now, Fintan watched her sleeping in the half-light. After the fever her face was all crumpled like a child's. Her hair, loose and damp with sweat, fell in large black curls.

Then, shortly before dawn, the very soft, slow motion began again. At first Fintan did not understand that it was the *Surabaya* once again under way. She slipped along the piers, towards the channel, towards Cape Coast, Accra, Keta, Lomé, Petit Popo, towards the estuary of the great Volta River, towards Cotonou, Lagos, towards the muddy waters of the river Ogun, towards the mouth of the rivers flowing with an ocean of mud at the estuary of the Niger River.

It was already morning. The hull of the *Surabaya* vibrated with the pulsation of the rods, the warm wind blew the smoke back over the stern, and Fintan's eyes stung with fatigue. On deck, as he leaned against the railing, he tried to see the gray sea, the ash-colored sea, the black coast fleeing behind them, enveloped in clouds of shrieking birds. Forward, on the cargo deck, Krus, Ghans, Yorubas, Ibos, and Doualas were still rolled up in their blankets, their heads cushioned against their bundles. The women were already awake, sitting on their heels, suckling their babies. There was the sound of children whining. In a few moments the men would pick up their sharp little hammers: the iron frames and the panels of the hatches with their eternal rust would begin to resonate as if the ship were a gigantic drum, a gigantic body shaking with the disordered throbbing of its multiple heart. And Maou was about to turn on her sweat-soaked berth, about to sigh, perhaps to call Fintan to fetch her a glass of water from the carafe on the mahogany night table. It was all so long, so slow, as they sailed their course across the endless sea, always different yet always the same.

In Cotonou, Maou and Fintan walked along the long sea wall which split the waves. In the port were many cargo ships, unloading. Farther away were the fishing boats, surrounded by pelicans.

Maou wore her voile dress, the one she had worn swimming in Takoradi. At the market in Lomé she bought a new straw hat. She wouldn't buy a cap. "They're for policemen," she said. Fintan refused to wear a hat. His straight chestnut hair, cut bluntly across his forehead, was like a cap. Since their swim in Takoradi he was reluctant to go on land. He stayed on deck with First Mate Heylings, who was overseeing the movement of goods.

The sky was low, a milky gray. The heat was torrid from earliest daylight. On the quay the dockers piled up crates of goods and prepared the ones which were to be loaded, bales of cotton, sacks of peanut. The

34

derricks hauled up nets full of merchandise. There was no one left on the cargo deck. The people had got off, the women with their babies held tight in their veils, bundles on their heads. There was a strange silence now, the frames and the hull of the ship had stopped their ringing, the engines had stopped; there remained only the continuous hum of the generator to work the derrick. Through the wide-open hatches you could see the hold, the dust rising, lit by electric bulbs.

"Maou, where are you going?"

"I'll be right back, my love."

Fintan watched with dread as she walked down the gangway, followed by the odious Gerald Simpson.

"Come on, we're going for a walk on the sea wall, we're going to visit the town."

Fintan didn't want to go. His throat was tight, he didn't really know why. Perhaps because one day it would be like this, he would have to go down the gangway, go into the town, and there would be that man waiting who would say: "I'm Geoffroy Allen, I'm your father. Come with me to Onitsha." This, too — to look at Maou's white silhouette, her white dress filling in the wind like a sail: she gave her arm to the Englishman, she listened to his declamations about Africa, the blacks, the jungle. It was unbearable. So Fintan shut himself in the window-less cabin, he switched on the night light, and he began to write a story in a little drawing book, with a thick pencil. First he wrote the title, in capital letters: A LONG JOURNEY.

Then he began the story:

ESTHER. ESTHER CAME TO AFRICA IN 1948.

SHE JUMPS ONTO THE DOCK AND WALKS IN THE FOREST.

It was good to write this story, locked in the cabin, so quiet, with the glow of the night light and the heat of the sun rising above the hull of the motionless ship.

THE BOAT IS CALLED NIGER. IT TAKES DAYS TO GO UP THE RIVER.

Fintan could feel the sun burning on his forehead, as it had long ago, in Saint-Martin. A spot of pain between his eyes. Grandmother Aurelia used to say it was his third eye, the eye he could use to see into the future. It was all so far away, so long ago. As if it had never existed. In the forest Esther walks in the midst of danger, watched by leopards and crocodiles. SHE ARRIVES IN ONITSHA. A HUGE HOUSE IS READY, WITH A MEAL AND A HAMMOCK. ESTHER LIGHTS A FIRE TO SCARE AWAY THE WILD ANIMALS. Time was a burn spreading slowly across Fintan's forehead, as in the old days when the summer sun rose very high above the valley of the Stura. Time had the bitter taste of quinine, the acrid smell of peanuts. Time was cold and damp like the prisoners' cells in Gorée. ESTHER WATCHES THE STORMS ABOVE THE FOREST. A BLACK MAN HAS BROUGHT HER A CAT. I AM HUNGRY, SAYS ESTHER. THEN I'LL GIVE YOU THIS CAT. TO EAT? NO, IN FRIENDSHIP. Night was coming, soothing the burning sun on Fintan's forehead. He heard Maou's voice in the corridor, Gerald Simpson's clipped accent. Outside, it was cool. Lightning streaked the sky in silence.

On the first-class deck Mr. Heylings sat bare-chested, wearing khaki shorts. He smoked as he watched the work of the derricks. "What are you doing here, Junge? Have you lost your mother?" He grabbed the boy by the head. His powerful hands squeezed Fintan's forehead and he lifted him very slowly until his feet left the ground. When Maou saw this, she cried out, "No! You're going to hurt my little boy!" The first mate laughed, swinging Fintan by the head. "It's good for them, ma'am, it makes them grow!"

Fintan slipped away. When he saw Mr. Heylings, he kept well away from him.

"Look, over there, it's the Porto Novo Canal. The first time I sailed through there I was very young. We were shipwrecked." He pointed towards the horizon, islands lost in the night. "Our captain had been drinking, you see, he ran the ship onto a sand bar, because of the tide. Our ship was blocking the entrance to the canal, nobody could get into Porto Novo! What a laugh!"

That evening there was a party on board the *Surabaya*. It was the birthday of Rosalind, the wife of one of the English officers. The captain had prepared everything. Maou was quite excited: "You know, Fintan, there's going to be dancing! There'll be music in the first-class lounge and everyone can go." Her eyes were shining. She looked like a schoolgirl. She hunted through her things for a long time, for a dress, a cardigan, shoes. She put on powder and rouge and combed her lovely hair for a long time.

It was dark by six. The Dutch sailors had rigged up strings of fairy lights. The *Surabaya* looked like a huge cake. There was no dinner that evening. In the large, red first-class lounge the armchairs had been pulled aside and a long table, covered in white tablecloths, had been prepared. On the table were bouquets of red flowers, baskets of fruit, bottles, trays of hors d'oeuvres, paper streamers, and, in one corner, a large fan which made a noise like an airplane.

Fintan stayed in the cabin, sitting on his berth, his exercise book lit by the night light.

"What are you doing?" asked Maou. She came over to look, but Fintan closed the exercise book.

"Nothing, nothing, it's my homework."

The pain in his forehead had ceased. The air was soft, light. The swell caused the ship to bob up and down against the dock. Africa was so far away; it was lost in the night, at the end of the pier, in all the channels and islands, engulfed by the rising tide. The waters of the river flowed quietly around the ship. Mr. Heylings came to get Maou. He was wearing his handsome white uniform with its stripes and a cap too small for his giant's head.

"You see, *Junge*"—that's what he always called Fintan, in his language—"we're already there, in the arms of the great Niger River, and the water flowing here is the river water. There's so much water in the Niger River that it takes the salt out of the sea, and when it rains, very far away near Gao in the desert, the sea here turns red, and tree trunks, even drowned animals, wash up on the beach."

Fintan looked down at the black water around the *Surabaya*, as if he might actually see drowned animals float by.

When the party had begun, Maou led Fintan into the first-class lounge, dazzling with lamps and strings of lights. There were bouquets on the tables, and flowers draped from the iron girders. The English officers, dressed in white, gathered around the Dutch captain, a heavy, bearded man with a flushed face. Despite the ventilator, which was turning at top speed, it was very hot, no doubt because of all the electric bulbs. Faces were bright with sweat. The women wore light, low-cut dresses and fanned themselves with Spanish fans bought in Dakar or with menus.

Near the long, flowered table stood the guests of honor, Colonel Metcalfe and his wife, Rosalind, very stiff in their ceremonial outfits. The Dutch stewards poured champagne and fruit juice. Maou led Fintan up to the buffet. She seemed overexcited, almost nervous.

"Come, my love, have something to eat."

"I'm not hungry, Maou."

"No, no, you must try some."

Music filled the lounge: an imposing phonograph played jazz records, the husky brilliance of Billie Holiday singing "Sophisticated Lady."

The English congregated in a tight circle around the Metcalfes. Maou threaded her way to the buffet, pulling Fintan by the hand. She looked like a little girl. The men were staring at her; Gerald Simpson whispered something into her ear. She was laughing. She had already had several glasses of champagne. Fintan was ashamed.

Maou gave him a paper plate with a strange, pale green fruit, cut in half around a large, obscene pit.

"Taste it, darling. I'll tell you what it is after you've tasted it, try it, you'll see how good it is."

Her eyes were shining. She had pulled her lovely hair up into a chignon, leaving wild tendrils on the nape of her neck; she wore red earrings. Her bare shoulders were the color of gingerbread.

"You'll see, Onitsha is a quiet little town, very pleasant. Stayed there briefly before the war. One of my good friends is there, Dr. Charon. Perhaps your husband has told you about him?"

The awful Simpson was declaiming, a glass of champagne level with his thin nose, as if he were sniffing the bubbles.

"Ah, the Niger, the longest river on earth," exclaimed Florizel, his face redder than a pepper.

"Excuse me, isn't it the Amazon, rather?" Simpson half turned towards the Belgian, his manner sarcastic. "I mean, the longest in Africa," rectified Florizel. He moved on, without listening to Simpson who said, in his grating voice, "Bad luck, it's the Nile." An English officer was waving his arms: ". . . hunting gorillas, in the hills of Oban, over by German Cameroon, I've got an entire collection of skulls at home, in Obudu. . . ." Voices spoke in English, Dutch, French. A tumult of voices, flooding, then ebbing, then rising again.

Fintan tasted the pale fruit from the edge of his spoon, disgusted, almost nauseated. "Taste it, darling, you'll see how good it is." The English officers shoved against the table, eating salad, hors d'oeuvres, drinking glasses of champagne. Perspiring women fanned themselves. The motor of the fan made its airplane noise, and the phonograph played Dixieland jazz. Above it all, from time to time, Mr. Heylings' laugh, his ogre's voice. Then someone began to play the piano, at the other end of the lounge. The Italian man danced with his nurse. Mr. Simpson took Maou by the arm; he was slightly drunk. In his high-pitched, almost accentless voice, he was telling jokes. Other English people arrived. They amused themselves by imitating the speech of the blacks, telling jokes in pidgin. Mr. Simpson pointed to the piano:

"Big black fellow box spose white man fight him, he cry too mus!"

Fintan had the insipid taste of the green fruit on his tongue. The lounge was awash in the smell of stale tobacco. Maou was laughing; she too was drunk. Her eyes shone, her bare shoulders shone in the glow of the strings of lights. Mr. Simpson held her by the waist. He had taken a big red flower from the table and pretended to give it to her, saying,

"Spose Missus catch di grass, he die."

The laughter echoed strangely, a barking sound. Now there was a circle around the awful Mr. Simpson. Even the Metcalfes had come over to hear the jokes in pidgin. The Englishman showed them an egg taken from the buffet table.

"Pickaninny stop along him fellow!" Others shouted, "Maïwot! Maï-wot!"

Fintan escaped to the deck. He was ashamed. He would have liked to take Maou with him out onto the deck. Then he felt the movement. It was only faint, a slight rocking, the muted vibration of the engines, the shudder of the waters along the hull. Outside the night was black; the strings of lights trailing from the derricks shone like stars.

To the fore the Dutch sailors were busy casting off the moorings. On the bridge stood First Mate Heylings, his white uniform glowing in the darkness.

Fintan ran to the end of the deck to see up forward. The cargo deck rose slowly on the swell. The channel buoys slid by, red to port, green to starboard, a flash every five seconds, and already the ocean wind was blowing, rattling the strings of lights, bringing this cool air, so soft, so powerful, which made one's heart beat faster. In the night there were still sounds of the party, the tinkling of the piano, the shrill voices of the women, laughter, applause. But they were far away, driven by the wind and the swell; the *Surabaya* sailed on, leaving the land, bound for other ports, other estuaries. They were headed for Port Harcourt, Calabar, Victoria.

As he leaned against the rail, Fintan could see the lights of Cotonou, already unreal, drowned in the horizon. Invisible islands went by; there was the terrifying sound of the sea on the reefs. The bow rose slowly across the waves.

Then, on the cargo deck darkened by the brilliance of the lanterns, Fintan discovered the blacks who had settled in for the trip. While the whites were partying in first class, they had come on board, silently; men, women, and children, carrying their bundles on their heads, walking one by one up the plank that served as a gangway. Watched over by the quartermaster, they had taken up their places on deck, between the rusted containers, against the frames of the bulwark, and they had waited noiselessly for the hour of departure. Perhaps a child had cried, or perhaps the old man with the thin face, his body covered in rags, had intoned his monotonous chant, his prayer. But the music from the lounge had hidden their voices, and they might have heard Mr. Simpson mocking them, imitating their language, and the English people shouting, "Maïwot! Maïwot!" and the story of "Pickaninny stop along him fellow!"

Fintan felt so angry, so ashamed that for a moment he wanted to go back to the first-class lounge. It was as if, in the night, all of the black people were looking at him, a sharp look, full of reproach. But the idea of going back into the huge room full of noise and the odor of stale tobacco was unbearable.

So Fintan went down to his cabin, lit the night light, and opened the little school exercise book where he had written, in large black letters, A LONG VOYAGE. And he began to write, thinking of the night, while the *Surabaya* headed for the open sea, weighted with light bulbs and music like a Christmas tree, slowly lifting her bow, an immense steel whale heading towards the Bay of Biafra with her load of sleeping black travellers.

On 13 April 1948, exactly one month after leaving the Gironde estuary, the *Surabaya* entered the harbor of Port Harcourt towards the end of a gray, rainy afternoon where heavy clouds clung to the shore. On the quay was a man, a stranger, tall and thin, his nose like an eagle's beak under a pair of steel spectacles, his thinning hair streaked with gray, dressed in a strange military raincoat that reached to his ankles over a pair of khaki trousers and those same shiny, black shoes that Fintan had already noticed on the feet of the English officers on board ship. The man kissed Maou, went up to Fintan, and shook his hand. Some distance beyond the customs buildings there was a large, emerald green Ford V8, dented and rusting, its windscreen crazed. Maou sat in front next to Geoffroy Allen, and Fintan climbed onto the rear seat among the boxes and suitcases. Rain streamed down the windows. There was lightning; night was approaching. The man turned around to Fintan and said, "Are you all right, boy?" The Ford began to roll down the track, towards Onitsha.

Onitsha

Fintan watched for lightning. He sat on the veranda and watched the sky above the river, where the storm was approaching. Every evening it was the same. At sunset the sky darkened to the west, towards Asaba, above Brokkedon Island. From the height of the terrace Fintan could survey the entire breadth of the river, could see the places where the tributaries—Anambara, Omerun—joined the river, and the large, flat island of Jersey, covered with reeds and trees. Downstream the river inscribed a slow curving line to the south, as vast as an arm of the sea, with the hesitant traces of small islands, like rafts adrift. The storm swirled. There were bloodied streaks in the sky, gaps in the clouds. Then, very rapidly, the black cloud went back up the river, chasing before it the flying ibises still lit by the sun.

Geoffroy's house was on a small hill overlooking the river, a short way upstream from the town of Onitsha, as if it were at the heart of an immense crossroads of water. At that moment the first rumblings of thunder could be heard, still far behind near the hills of Ihni and Munshi, in the forest. The earth shook. It was very hot, and the air was very close.

The first time, Maou had hugged Fintan to her, so hard that he felt her heart beating against his ear. "I'm frightened, count with me, Fintan, count the seconds. . . ." She explained that the sound rushed to catch up with the light, at one thousand seventy-two feet a second.

"Count, Fintan, one, two, three, four, five . . ." Before ten the thunder boomed beneath the ground, echoing through the house, causing the floor beneath their feet to tremble. "Two miles," said Fintan. And, immediately, other bright columns of light crossed the sky, sharply illuminating the water of the great river, the waves, the islands, the black line of the palm trees. "Count, one, two, no, more slowly than that, three, four, five . . ."

The lightning increased, shattering the clouds, then the rain began to fall on the tin roof, separate drops at first, like little pebbles rolling down the fluting, and the sound grew, exploding magnificently, terrifying. Fintan could feel his heart beating faster. In the shelter of the veranda he watched the dark curtain moving up the river, just like a cloud, and the bursts of lightning no longer illuminated the shore or the islands. Everything was swallowed, disappearing into the water of the sky, the water of the river; everything was drowned.

Motionless beneath the veranda, Fintan could not look away. Transfixed, shivering. Trying to breathe, as if the cloud were moving through his body, filling his lungs.

The pandemonium was all around him, as high as the sky. The water streamed from the tin roof in powerful spurts, washing over the ground, down the hill to the river. There was nothing else, only the falling, flowing water.

Shouts broke through the tumult, rousing Fintan from his stupor. Children were running in the garden, on the road, their black bodies shining in the bursts of lightning. They called out the name of the rain: "Ozoo! Ozoo!" There were other voices, inside the house. Elijah the cook and Maou rushed through the house, buckets in their hands, to mop up. The metal roof was leaking everywhere. The rusted iron of the veranda roof began to sag beneath the weight of the water, and the rain burst into the rooms, blood-colored. Geoffroy appeared on the veranda, bare-chested, soaked from head to foot; his gray hair was plastered in streaks on his forehead, and the lenses of his glasses had fogged up. Fintan looked at him and did not understand. "Come, don't stay outside." Maou led Fintan to the rear of the house, into the kitchen, the only room where the water had not entered. Her face was expressionless. Her clothes, too, were soaked; she seemed frightened. Fintan drew her to him. He counted for her, slowly, between each blinding flash, "One, two, three, four . . ." A moment later he could only reach three: the burst of thunder shook the earth and the house. Everything made of glass seemed to shatter. Maou's hands were pressed against her face, her palms hard against her eyes.

Then the storm passed. It moved on up the length of the river, headed towards the hills. Fintan went back out on the terrace. The islands were visible again, long and low, like prehistoric animals. The night was forgotten; there was a gray, crepuscular light. You could see inside the house; you could see the fields of grass, the palm branches, the line of the river. Suddenly it was very hot, the air heavy and motionless. Vapor rose from the drenched earth. The rolling of thunder had disappeared. Fintan listened to the voices, the shouts of the children, calling, "Waa! Waa!" He heard barking, too, in the distance towards the town.

With nightfall came the croaking of the toads. Maou shuddered when she heard Geoffroy starting the motor of the V8. Geoffroy shouted something: he was going to check the warehouses; the rain had flooded the docks.

The children had left the house behind; you could still hear their voices, but they were invisible, hidden in the night. Fintan stepped down from the terrace and began to walk in the sodden grass. The lightning was far away now; from time to time there was a faint glow above the trees, but the rumbling of thunder could no longer be heard. Mud sucked at his feet. Fintan took his shoes off and tied them round his neck with the laces, like a wild man.

He moved into the night, through the vast garden. Maou was lying in the hammock, in the large empty room. She shivered with fever and could not keep her eyes open. The light of the oil lamp on the little table burned her eyelids. She felt the loneliness: it was like a hollow space deep within, a space she could not fill. Or perhaps it was the amebiasis that had weakened her, two months after their arrival in Onitsha. She felt an extreme hardness, a painful lucidity. She knew what was inside her, what was eating its way into her, and she could do nothing. She recalled each moment since her arrival in Onitsha—settling into the big, empty house, nothing but these wooden walls and this tin roof resting upon a framework that vibrated with every storm. The hammocks, the narrow trestle beds, under the mosquito nets, like in a dormitory. And above all there was the uneasiness—this man who had become a stranger, his face grown hard, his hair now gray, his thin body, the color of his skin. The happiness of which she had dreamt on the deck of the *Surabaya* did not exist here. There was also the way Fintan looked at his father—a look full of wariness and instinctive hatred—and Geoffroy's cold anger each time Fintan defied him.

Now, in the slowly returning silence of the night, broken only by the chirring of insects and the voices of toads, Maou swung in her hammock, watching the light of the lamp. She sang softly in Italian, a nursery rhyme, a *ritornello*. She broke off, took her hands from her face, and said, just once, without raising her voice, "Fintan?"

She heard the echo of her voice in the empty house. Geoffroy was at the wharf, Elijah had gone home. But Fintan? She did not dare climb out of the hammock to walk to the little room at the end of the corridor, to see the empty hammock hanging in the middle of the room from the rings attached to the wall. And the window with the shutters open to the black night.

She remembered how fervent her hopes had been for this new life:

50

Onitsha, this unknown world, where nothing would be like anything she had experienced—not the things, not the people, not the odors, not the color of the sky—not even the taste of water. That might have been because of the filter, the big cylinder of white porcelain that Elijah filled every morning with the well water which flowed so fine and white from the brass tap. Then she had fallen ill, she thought she would die of the fever and diarrhea, and now the filter with its tasteless water horrified her. She dreamt of fountains, of frozen streams, like in Saint-Martin.

And there was the name, the name she had repeated every day, during the war, in Saint-Martin, in Santa Anna, then in Nice and Marseilles, the name like a key to all her dreams. So every day she had Fintan say it, secretly, so that Grandmother Aurelia and Aunt Rosa would not hear it. He looked so serious that it almost intimidated her, or else gave her the giggles. "When we get to Onitsha . . ." He would say, "Is it like this, in Onitsha?" But he never spoke of Geoffroy, he never wanted to say "my father." He thought it was not true. Geoffroy was simply a strange man who wrote letters.

And then she had decided to leave, to go there and join him. She had got everything ready, carefully, without a word to anyone, not even Aurelia. There were the passports to have done, money to be found for the boat tickets. She had gone to Nice to sell her jewelry—a gold watch that had belonged to her father and some gold louis given to her before her wedding. Grandmother Aurelia did not speak of Geoffroy Allen. He was an Englishman, an enemy. Aunt Rosa was more talkative; she liked to say, "Porco inglese." She thought it was fun to have Fintan say it, when he was small. She had admired Don Benito, even when he had gone mad and sent all the young men off to be butchered. Fintan repeated after her, "Porco inglese!" laughing hysterically. He was five years old. It was their secret, his and Rosa's. One day Maou heard them; she looked at the old maid and her eyes were like two blue blades. "Don't ever make Fintan say that again, or I'll leave at once and take him with me." She had nowhere to go. Aunt Rosa knew that perfectly well, she paid no attention to Maou's threats. The flat just under the roof, number 18, rue des Accoules, had only two rooms and a narrow kitchen painted yellow which gave on to a well of light.

Maou broke the news to them barely a month before the departure. Aurelia went all pale. She said nothing because she knew it was no use. She asked: "And Fintan?"

"We are both leaving."

Maou knew that Grandmother Aurelia was more sorry about Fintan than about herself. She knew they would probably not see her again. Rosa, on the other hand, did not care. It was just pique, her hatred of the *inglese*. And so she talked endlessly, a flood of insane, black words, words of acid.

Maou stood for a long time on the threshold of the small building, holding the woman who had been her mother. There were people in the street, a tumult of voices, children's cries, swifts calling. It was the beginning of summer. It was not yet night. The train was due to leave for Bordeaux at seven.

At the last moment, when the taxi had pulled up, Aurelia could no longer bear it. She was choking. She blurted, "I'll come with you to Bordeaux, please let me!" Maou pushed her away, harshly, "No, that wouldn't be reasonable." Fintan breathed the odor of his grandmother's clothes and hair. He did not really understand. He dodged past her and pushed her away. He had closed his mind against it. What was that supposed to mean, "Au revoir," when they would never meet again?

He had never seen so much space. Ibusun, Geoffroy's house, was located outside the town, upstream, above the mouth of the Omerun, where the reeds began. On the other side of the small hill, towards the rising sun, there was an immense prairie of yellow grass which stretched out of sight in the direction of the Ihni and Munshi hills, where the clouds were caught. During a reception the new D.O., Gerald Simpson, had told Maou that over there in those hills the last lowland gorillas were hiding. He had pulled Maou over to the window of the Residency, where one could see the blue mass against the horizon. Geoffroy had shrugged his shoulders. But for that reason Fintan liked to go to the edge of the field of grass. The hills were always dark, mysterious.

At dawn, before even Geoffroy was up, Fintan would set off on the barely visible path. Before coming to the Omerun there was a sort of clearing, then the path led to a sandy beach. It was there that the local women went to bathe and do their washing. Bony had shown the spot to Fintan. It was a secret place, full of laughter and singing, a place where boys were not to show their faces if they did not want to be assailed with shouts of abuse and blows. The women went into the water, untying their dresses; they sat and talked together while the stream flowed around them. Then they would tie their dresses around their hips and wash their laundry by slapping it against the flat rocks.

Their shoulders shone, their long breasts swung to the rhythm of their slapping. In the morning it was almost cold. Mist moved slowly down the stream to where it met the big river, touching the treetops, swallowing the islands. It was a magical moment.

Bony was a fisherman's son. He had come several times to offer Maou fish or young she-goats. He had waited for Fintan behind the house, at the edge of the big field of yellow grass. His real name was Josip, or Josef, but because he was tall and thin they called him Bony. His face was smooth, his eyes were intelligent and full of laughter. Fintan immediately became his friend. He spoke pidgin and also a bit of French, because his maternal uncle was a Douala. He had a number of set phrases, "good show old bean," "hello old chap," "dash it all," things like that. He knew all kinds of curses and swearwords in English; he taught Fintan what "cunt" meant and other things whose meaning he did not know. He could also speak in sign language. Fintan quickly learned to speak the same language.

Bony knew everything about the river and the surrounding area. He could run as fast as a dog, barefoot through the tall grass. In the beginning Fintan wore the big, black shoes and woollen socks the Englishmen wore. Dr. Charon had insisted to Maou, "You know, this isn't France here. There are scorpions, snakes, poisonous thorns. I know what I'm talking about. In Afikpo six months ago a D.O. died of gangrene because he thought that in Africa one could walk about barefoot in sandals, as if he were in Brighton." But one day, when he wasn't watching where he was walking, Fintan got his socks full of red ants. They found a niche in among the stitches, their jaws in such a ferocious vice that when he tried to pull off the socks their heads remained in his skin. From that day on Fintan no longer wanted to wear either socks or shoes.

Bony made him touch the soles of his feet, hard as a leather sole.

Fintan hid the wretched socks in his hammock, put the big black shoes in the metal wardrobe, and walked barefoot through the grass.

At dawn the yellow prairie seemed immense. The paths were invisible. Bony knew the way among the mud puddles and thorny bushes. Partridges shot up, screeching. In the clearings they flushed out flocks of guinea fowl. Bony knew how to imitate bird calls with leaves, reeds, or even just his finger in his mouth.

He was a good hunter and yet there were certain animals he did not want to kill. One day Geoffroy went out into the clearing in front of the house. The hens were squawking because a falcon was tracing circles above them in the sky. Geoffroy placed his rifle on his shoulder, fired, and the bird fell. Bony was at the entrance to the garden and saw everything. He was angry; his eyes no longer laughed. He pointed to the empty sky, to where the falcon had been tracing its circles. "Him god!" It's a god, he said repeatedly. He said the bird's name, "Ugo." Fintan felt ashamed and frightened. It was so strange: Ugo was a god, and it was also the name of Bony's grandmother; Geoffroy had killed Ugo. For that reason too Fintan no longer wanted to wear the black shoes to run through the plain of grass. They were *porco inglese* shoes.

At the edge of the plain there was a sort of clearing of red earth. Fintan had come across it all alone, the first days he had adventured that far. It was the city of termites.

The termitaries were built like chimneys, straight into the sky, some of them taller than Fintan, in the center of a patch of bare, sun-cracked earth. A strange silence reigned over this city, and without knowing why, Fintan picked up a stick and began to strike the termites' nests. Perhaps it was fear, the loneliness of this silent city. The chimneys of hardened earth resounded as if under cannon fire. The stick bounced, struck again. Gradually breaches began to appear at the top of the nests. Whole sections of wall crumbled into dust, laying bare the tunnels and galleries, scattering onto the ground the pale larvae to writhe in the red earth.

Fintan had attacked the termitaries one after the other, wildly. Sweat ran off his forehead, into his eyes, down his shirt. He no longer knew very clearly what he was doing. Perhaps it was to forget, to destroy. To reduce his own image to powder. To obliterate Geoffroy's face, the cold anger that shone at times in the circles of his eyeglasses.

Bony arrived. Ten or more nests were eviscerated. Some sections of wall remained standing, like ruins, where the larvae wriggled in the light of the sun among the blind termites. Fintan was sitting on the ground, his hair and clothes red with dust, his hands aching from his efforts. Bony looked at him. Fintan would never be able to forget that look. It was the same anger as the time Geoffroy Allen had killed the falcon. "You ravin' mad, you crazy!" He had taken the earth and the termite larvae in his hands. "This is god!" He repeated it in pidgin, with the same dark look. The termites were the guardians of the grasshoppers; without them the world would be ravaged. Fintan had felt the same shame. For weeks Bony did not come to Ibusun. Fintan went to wait for him down by the first ruined pier, hoping to see him go by on his father's long pirogue.

Before the rains the sun was burning. The afternoons seemed endless, without a breath of air. Nothing moved. Maou would lie down on the camp bed in the hallway, because the cool cement walls protected from the heat. Geoffroy came back late, there were always things to be done at the wharf—deliveries of merchandise, meetings at the Club, at Simpson's. When he came home, overwhelmed by fatigue, he would lock himself away in his study and sleep until six or seven. Maou had dreamt of Africa, of long rides on horseback through the bush, of the hoarse cries of wild beasts in the evening, of the deep forests rich with flowers both shimmering and poisonous, paths leading to mystery. She had not thought it would be like this, the long monotony of the days, waiting on the veranda, and the town with its tin roofs boiling with heat. She had not imagined Geoffroy Allen to be this employee of the commercial companies of West Africa, spending the larger part of his time drawing up the inventory of crates newly arrived from England with soap, toilet paper, tins of corned beef, and sacks of flour. Wild beasts did not exist, except as an object of bragging on the part of officers, and the forest had disappeared long before to leave room for the fields of yams and plantations of oil palms.

Nor had Maou imagined the gatherings at the D.O.'s place, each week, the men in khaki with their black shoes and their woollen knee socks, standing on the terrace, whiskey glass in hand, talking about the office; and their wives in pale dresses and court shoes, talking about their problems with their maids. One afternoon, less than a month after her arrival, Maou went with Geoffroy to Gerald Simpson's. He lived in a big wooden house not far from the docks, a fairly dilapidated house that he was in the process of renovating. He had got the idea in his head to dig a swimming pool in his garden, for the club members.

It was tea time, and the heat was sweltering. The black workers were prisoners that Simpson had obtained through Rally, the Resident, because he couldn't find anyone else, or because he did not want to pay them. The workers arrived at the same time as the guests, bound by a long chain that was linked by rings to their left ankle; in order not to fall they had to walk in step, as if on parade.

Maou was on the terrace and watched with astonishment—these chained men were crossing the garden, their shovels on their shoulder, with a regular noise each time the rings around their ankles pulled on the chain—left, left. Their black skin shone through their rags like metal. Some looked over towards the terrace; their faces were eroded by fatigue and suffering.

Then the meal was served in the shade of the veranda—huge dishes of foufou and grilled mutton, glasses of guava juice filled with crushed ice. On the long table there was a white tablecloth and bouquets of flowers ordered by the Resident's wife herself. The guests spoke loudly, roared with laughter, but Maou could not take her eyes off the group of convicts, who were beginning to dig into the earth at the other end of the garden. Their guards had released them from the long chain, but they were still hindered by the rings around their ankles. With pick and shovel they hacked at the hard earth, there where Simpson would have his swimming pool. It was terrifying. Maou could hear nothing else, nothing but the hammering against the hard earth, the sound of the convicts' breathing, the clanking of the rings around their ankles.

She felt her throat tighten, as if she might cry. She looked at the English officers around the table, so white; she sought Geoffroy's gaze. But no one was paying any attention to her, and the women continued to eat and to laugh. Gerald Simpson's gaze paused a moment upon her. There was a strange glint in his eyes, behind the lenses of his glasses. He wiped his little blond moustache with a napkin. Maou felt such hatred that she had to avert her gaze.

At the end of the garden, near the grille which acted as a fence, the black men were burning beneath the sun, sweat glistening on their backs, on their shoulders. And, always, the sound of their breathing, a hunh! of pain each time they struck the earth.

Suddenly, Maou got up, and in a voice trembling with anger, with her strange French and Italian accent in English, she said: "But you must give them something to eat and drink, look, these poor fellows, they are hungry and thirsty!" She used the word "fellow," the pidgin term.

There was a stunned silence. For a very long minute all the guests' faces turned towards her, staring at her, and she saw that even Geoffroy was stunned as he watched her, his face red, his mouth drooping at the corners, his closed fists pressing on the table.

Gerald Simpson was the first to regain his senses, saying, simply, "Ah yes, quite right, I suppose . . ."

He called the boy, he gave orders. In an instant the guards had led the convicts out of sight, behind the house. The D.O. then said, looking at Maou ironically, "Well, that's better now, isn't it, they were making a wretched noise, we shall have a bit of a rest ourselves now too."

The guests laughed halfheartedly. The men continued to speak, drink their coffee, and smoke their cigars, sitting in their wicker chairs at the end of the veranda. The women remained around the table, chattering with Mrs. Rally.

Then Geoffroy seized Maou by the arm and took her home in the V8, driving very quickly along the deserted track. He did not say a single word about the convicts. But after that he never again asked Maou to accompany him to the D.O.'s or to the Resident's. And whenever Gerald Simpson met Maou by chance, in the street or on the wharf, he greeted her very coldly, his steel blue gaze expressing nothing — as it should be — beyond a barely perceptible disdain.

The sun baked the red earth. Bony showed Fintan: he went to fetch the reddest earth, from the banks of the Omerun, and brought it back, all wet, in an old pair of trousers with knotted legs. In a clearing, in the shade of a small grove, the children cut up the earth and made small statuettes which they placed in the sun to dry. They made vases, plates, cups, and figures too, masks, dolls. Fintan made animals — horses, elephants, a crocodile. Bony tended to make men and women standing on an earthen base, with a twig for their spinal cord and dry grass for their hair. He sculpted their features with precision: almond-shaped eyes, nose, mouth, fingers and toes as well. For the men he made a rising sex, and for the women, nipples and a pubis, a triangle split in the middle. It made them laugh.

One day, urinating together in the tall grass, Fintan had seen Bony's sex, long, ending with a red tip like a wound. It was the first time he had ever seen a circumcised sex.

Bony urinated squatting down, like a girl. Because Fintan remained standing he made fun of him. He had said, "Cheese." Afterwards, he used to repeat that a lot, when Fintan did something he didn't like. "What does 'cheese' mean, Maou?" "It means 'fromage' in English." But that was no real explanation. Later, Bony said that uncircumcised penises were always dirty, that under the little skin there was something that looked like cheese.

The afternoons drifted with the sun along the cement terrace. Fintan brought home the statuettes and the cooking pots, and he looked at them for so long that everything seemed to grow black and scorched, not unlike shadows on snow.

Clouds gathered above the islands. When the shade reached Jersey and Brokkedon, Fintan knew the rain was near. That is when Asaba, the town on the opposite shore (named for the snake) where the noise of the sawmills came from, would turn on its electric lights. The rain began to fall on the cement on the terrace, so hot that vapor rose instantly into the air. Scorpions fled to the holes between the stones, under the foundation. Thick drops fell on the pottery, on the statues, splattering blood stains. Cities collapsed, entire cities with their houses, their ponds, the statues of their gods. The last god, because he was the tallest, the one Bony called Orun, remained standing among the ruins. His backbone stuck out from his back, his sex was disappearing, his face was gone. "Orun, Orun!" cried Fintan. Bony said that Shango had killed the sun. He said that Jakuta, the stone thrower, had buried the sun. He showed Fintan how to dance in the rain, with a body shining like metal, feet red with the blood of men.

Strange, terrifying things happened at night. You did not know exactly what, you could not see, but something lurked around the house, it walked outside, in the grass in the garden, and farther away, near the hillside, in the swamps of the Omerun. Bony said it was Oya, mother of the waters. He said it was Asaba, the big snake that lives in the faults in the earth, on the side of the rising sun. You had to speak to them, softly, in the night, and not forget to leave them a gift, hidden in the grass on a plantain leaf — fruit, bread, even money.

Geoffroy Allen was absent and he came home late. He went to Gerald Simpson's, to the judge's home, to a grand reception at the Residency to honor the commanding officer of the Sixth Battalion of Enugu. He met other representatives of the trading companies — the Commercial Company of West Africa, Jackel & Co., Ollivant, Chanrai & Co., John Holt & Co, African Oil Nuts. These names were strange to Fintan, when Geoffroy spoke to Maou; names of strange people, who bought and sold, who sent purchase notes, telegrams, orders. There was one name above all, United Africa; Fintan had seen it on the parcels Geoffroy sent to France — jam from South Africa, boxes of tea, of brown sugar. In Onitsha the name was everywhere, on the paper in Geoffroy's office, on the black metal trunks, on the copper plates on the walls of buildings on the wharf. On the boat which came each week to deliver the mail and supplies.

At night the rain fell gently on the tin roof, sliding along the gutters, filling the great drums painted in red over which screens of grayish brown canvas were stretched to prevent mosquitoes from laying their eggs. It was the song of the water, Fintan remembered, back then, in Saint-Martin; he would dream with his eyes open under the pale mosquito net, watching the flickering flame of the punkah lamp. On the walls, transparent lizards would shoot forward, suddenly, then settle down with a tiny squeak of satisfaction.

Fintan listened for the sound of the V8 coming up the steep stone path to the house. Sometimes, in the grass, there were the hoarse cries of wild cats chasing their cat, Mollie, or the indiscreet hooting of an owl in the trees, the whining cry of the nightjars. It seemed to him at that moment that there was nothing anywhere else, that there had never been anything other than the river, the shacks with their tin roofs, this big empty house peopled with scorpions and moths, and the immense expanse of grass where the night spirits wandered. That is what he had thought of when he climbed into the train and the station platform had pulled away, carrying Grandmother Aurelia and Aunt Rosa with it, like old dolls. Then in the cabin of the *Surabaya*, when he began to write the story A LONG VOYAGE, with the piercing sound of the hammers on the rusted ribs.

Now he knew that he was in the very heart of his dream, in the most burning, pungent place, like the place in his body where all the blood ebbed and flowed.

At night there was the beating of drums. It began towards the end of the afternoon when the men returned from work and Maou was sitting on the veranda, reading or writing in her language. Fintan lay down on the floor, bare chested because of the heat. He went down the steps and swung from the trapeze bar Geoffroy had hung up under the roof of the veranda. He entertained himself by lifting the carpet at the foot of the stairs with a twig to watch the scorpions wriggling. Sometimes there was a female, her young clinging to her back.

There were streaks in the darkening sky, and when you were not quite aware there would be a sudden rolling of drums, both far away and muffled, and at the same time you realized that it had begun a good while ago, on the other side of the big river, in Asaba perhaps, closer now, stronger, insistent, coming from the east from the village of Omerun; and Maou raised her head, trying to hear.

At night it was a strange noise, very soft, a palpitation, a gentle rustling, as if to calm the violence of the thunderclaps. Fintan liked to hear the drumming — he thought of Orun, of the Lord Shango; it was for them that the men made this music.

The first time Fintan had heard the drums, he had clung to Maou, because she was frightened. She had said something, to reassure herself. "There's a celebration in the village, listen. . . ." Or perhaps she had said nothing, because this wasn't like thunder, you couldn't count the seconds. Nearly every evening there was this light thrumming, a voice which came from everywhere, from the river Omerun, from the hills, the town, even the sawmill at Asaba. It was the end of the rainy season, the lightning was ending.

Maou was alone with Fintan. Geoffroy always came home so late. When she thought that Fintan was asleep in his bed, Maou would leave the hammock and walk barefoot through the big empty house, lighting her way with the electric torch because of the scorpions. On the veranda there was only the flickering light of a night light. Maou sat in an armchair at the end of the terrace to try and see the town and the river. The lights shone above the water, and when there was another flash of lightning she could see the surface of the water, hard and smooth like metal, and the ghostly foliage of the trees. She shivered, but not from fear, from fever rather, the bitter taste of quinine in her body.

66

She would wait for each sudden change in the quiet sound of the drums. In the silence the night shone even brighter. Around Ibusun the insects whirred, the loud croaking of the toads grew louder still, then they too stopped. Maou stayed there for a long time, perhaps hours, without moving from her rattan armchair. She wasn't thinking about anything. She was remembering, that was all. The child growing inside her; the waiting, in Fiesole; the silence. The letters from Africa which did not arrive. Fintan's birth, the departure for Nice. There was no more money, she had had to work, sewing at home, cleaning houses. The war. Geoffroy had written only one letter, to say he was going to cross the Sahara to Algiers in order to come and get her. Then nothing more. The Germans were after Cameroon; they were blockading the seas. Before leaving for Saint-Martin she had received a message, a book left in front of her door. It was Margaret Mitchell's novel, from the year they had met in Fiesole; she took it everywhere with her, a hardbound book covered in blue cloth, printed in very fine characters. When Geoffroy had left for Africa she had given it to him and now it was there, in front of her door, a message from nowhere. She had said nothing to either Aurelia or Rosa. She was too frightened that they might tell her it meant the Englishman had died, somewhere, in Africa.

The toads' cries, the insects' chirring, the tireless beating of the drums on the other side of the river. It was a different music. Maou looked at her hands, moving each finger. She remembered the keyboard of the piano at Livorno, heavy and ornate, like a catafalque. That was so long ago. At night, the faraway sounds of the piano might come back. When she had arrived that first week in Onitsha, it was with joy that she had discovered the Club's piano in the big hall adjacent to District Officer Simpson's house, where the English would go to sit and read, endlessly, their *Nigeria Gazette* and their *African Advertiser*. She had sat down on the stool, she had blown away the red dust clinging to the cover, and she had played a few notes, a few bars from *Gymnopédies* or

Gnossiennes. The sound of the piano rang out as far as the garden. She had turned around, had seen all those motionless faces, had felt their eyes upon her, the icy silence. The black waiters of the Club had paused on the threshold, frozen with surprise. Not only had a woman come into the Club, but on top of it she was playing music! Maou had left, red with shame and anger; she had walked quickly, then run through the dusty streets of the town. She remembered Gerald Simpson's voice, on the boat, imitating the blacks: "Spose Missus he fight black fellow he cry too mus!" Some time later she went as far as the door of the Club to fetch Geoffroy, and she saw that the black piano had disappeared. In its place there was a table and a bouquet, probably the work of Mrs. Rally.

She would wait in the night, her hands pressed against her face to keep from seeing the flickering glow of the lamp. At night, when all human noises ceased, there remained the quiet beating of intermittent drums, and she thought she could hear the sound of the big river, like the sea. Or was it the memory of the sound of waves at San Remo, in the room with the half open shutters. The sea at night, when it was too hot to sleep. She had wanted to show Geoffroy the region where she was born, Fiesole, in the gentle hills near Florence. She knew very well that she would find nothing left, no one, not even the memory of her father and mother, whom she had never known. Perhaps it was for that reason that Geoffroy had chosen her, because she was alone, because, unlike him, she had no family to renounce. Grandmother Aurelia, in Livorno, in Genoa, had been no more than a nanny, and Aunt Rosa had never been Aurelia's sister, only a mean, embittered, old maid with whom Aurelia shared her life. Maou had met Geoffroy Allen in the spring of 1935, in Nice, where he was travelling, having completed his engineering studies in London. He was tall, thin, romantic, penniless, and without a family, like her, since he had moved away from his parents. She was mad about him, and she had followed him to Italy, to San

Remo, to Florence. She was only eighteen, but she was already used to deciding everything on her own. She had wanted this child right away, for herself, not to be alone anymore, without a word to anyone.

It was good to think of that time, in the silence of the night. She remembered what he used to tell her then, his urge to go away, to Egypt, the Sudan, to go as far as Meroë, to follow the path. He spoke of little else — the last kingdom of the Nile, the black queen who had crossed the desert to the heart of Africa. He spoke of it as if nothing on earth at the present time had any importance, as if the light of legend shone brighter than the visible sun.

At the end of the summer, as the child was already growing in Maou's belly, they were married. Aurelia gave her permission, for well she knew that nothing could stop Maou. But Rosa said, "*Porco inglese,*" because she, who had found no one to marry her, was jealous.

Geoffroy Allen left immediately for West Africa, for the Niger River. He applied for a position with the United Africa Company, and he was hired. He was going to do business there, buying and selling, and above all he would be able to follow the course of his dream, to go back in time to the place where the queen of Meroë had founded her new city.

Maou kept all his letters. She was overcome by such a thrill of enthusiasm that she read them out loud, alone in her room in Nice.

There was war in Spain, in Eritrea, the world had gone mad, but nothing was of any importance. Geoffroy was out there, on the banks of the big river; he was going to discover the secret of the last queen of Meroë. He was preparing Maou's journey; he said, "When we are together again in Onitsha . . ." Aunt Rosa grumbled, "*Porco inglese,* he's crazy! Instead of coming to look after you! With the child on the way!" The child was born in March; Maou wrote a long letter at that time, practically a novel, to tell him everything — the birth, the name she had chosen because of Ireland, their life to come. But the reply was slow in coming. There were strikes, things were getting worse. There was not enough money. There was more and more talk of war, there were marches in the streets of Nice, against the Jews; the newspapers were full of hatred.

When Italy went to war, they had to flee from Nice and find refuge in the mountains, in Saint-Martin. Because of Geoffroy they had to hide and change their names. There was talk of prison camps where the English were held, in Borgo San Dalmazzo.

There was no longer any future. Only silence, daily, consuming history. Maou thought of the black queen of Meroë, of the impossible journey across the desert. Why wasn't Geoffroy here?

Those were long-ago, foreign years. Now Maou had reached the river, she had come, finally, to the country she had dreamt of for so long. And everything was so ordinary. Ollivant, Chanrai, United Africa—was it for those names that she had come?

Africa burns like a secret, like a fever. Geoffroy Allen cannot tear his eyes away, not even for a moment; he cannot dream another dream. It is the face sculpted with the marks of the *itsi*, the masked face of the Umundri. In the morning they wait on the quays of Onitsha, immobile, balancing on one leg, like scorched statues, Chuku's envoys on earth.

It is for them that Geoffroy has remained in this town, despite the horror inspired in him by the offices of the United Africa, despite the Club, despite the Resident and his wife, their dogs who eat nothing but beef filet and sleep under mosquito nets. Despite the climate, despite the routine of the wharf. Despite separation from Maou, and the son born far away whom he did not watch grow up, for whom he is nothing but a stranger.

But they are there every day, on the quay, from dawn, waiting for who knows what, a pirogue to carry them upstream or bring them a mysterious message. Then they leave, they disappear, walking through the tall grass, to the east, on the road to Awgu and Owerri. Geoffroy tries to speak to them, a few words of Ibo, phrases in Yoruba, in pidgin, but they are always silent, not haughty, merely absent, disappearing rapidly in single file along the river, lost to view in the tall grass yellowed by drought. They are the Umundri, the Ndinze, the "ancestors," the "initiated." The people of Chuku, the Sun, circled by his halo as a father is circled by his children.

It is the *itsi* sign. That is what Geoffroy saw on the faces when he first arrived in Onitsha. The sign carved into the skin of the men's faces, like writing upon stone. It is the sign which entered him, touched his heart, marked him, too, on his too white face, on his skin where from birth there has never been the mark of the burn. But now he feels this burn, this secret. Men and women of the Umundri people, in the streets of Onitsha; absurd shadows wandering in the alleyways of red dust, among the acacia groves, with their herds of goats and their dogs. Only some of them wear on their faces the sign of their ancestor Ndri, the sign of the sun.

Around them there is silence. One day however an old man called Moises, who remembers Aro Chuku and the oracle, told Geoffroy the story of the first Eze Ndri, in Aguleri: at that time, he said, there was nothing to eat, and men were forced to eat earth and grass. And so Chuku, the sun, sent Eri and Namaku down from heaven. But Ndri was not sent from the sky. He had to wait on an anthill, because the earth was nothing but a swamp. He lamented, Why do my brothers have food? Chuku sent a man from Awka, with tools from the forge—bellows and a grate with its embers—and the man was able to dry the earth. Eri and Namaku were fed by Chuku, they ate what is known as the Azu Igwe, the back of the sky. Those who ate it never slept.

Then Eri died, and Chuku stopped sending Azu Igwe, the back of the sky. Ndri was hungry, moaning. Chuku said, Obey me without thinking, and you will receive your food. What must I do? asked Ndri. Chuku said, You must kill your oldest son and daughter and bury them. Ndri answered, What you ask of me is terrible, I cannot do it. And so Chuku sent Dioka to Ndri, and Dioka was the father of the initiated, the one who had carved the first *itsi* sign upon their faces. And Dioka marked the faces of the children. And Chuku said to Ndri, Now, do what I ordered of you. And Ndri killed his children and for them he dug two graves. Three weeks of four days went by, and young sprouts appeared upon their graves. On the grave of his oldest son Ndri unearthed a yam. He had it cooked and he ate it, and it was excellent. Then he fell into a deep sleep, so deep that everyone believed he was dead.

The next day, from his daughter's tomb, Ndri unearthed a koko root; he ate it and fell asleep again. For this reason the yam is called son of Ndri and the koko root is called daughter of Ndri.

This is why, even today, the Eze Ndri must mark the face of his oldest son and daughter with the *itsi* sign, in memory of the first children who, through their death, brought food to man.

Something opens up at that moment in Geoffroy's heart. It is the sign branded upon the skin of the face, etched with a knife and dusted with copper. The sign which makes young men and women the children of the sun.

On the forehead, the signs of the sun and moon.

On the cheeks, the plumes of the wings and tail of a falcon.

The drawing of the sky, so that those who receive it no longer know fear, no longer fear suffering. The sign which liberates those who wear it. Enemies can no longer kill them, the English can no longer chain them together and make them work. They are Chuku's creatures, the children of the sun.

Suddenly Geoffroy feels a dizziness. He knows why he has come here, to this city, to this river. As if the secret has always been burning inside him. As if everything he has lived and dreamt is as nothing before the sign etched on the forehead of the last Aros.

It was the red season, the season of a wind which cracked the banks of the river. Fintan ventured farther and farther, aimlessly. When he had finished working on his English and his sums with Maou, he would dash off through the field of grass and go down to the Omerun. Beneath his bare feet the earth was parched and cracked, the bushes blackened by the sun. He listened to the sound of his feet drumming beneath him in the silence of the savannah.

At noon the sky was naked; there were no more clouds above the hills to the east. On rare occasions, at twilight, the clouds would puff up towards the sea. The plain of grass seemed to be an ocean of dryness. When he ran, the long hard blades whipped against his face and hands. There was no other sound, only his heels thudding on the ground, his heart beating in his throat, the rasping of his breath.

Now Fintan had learned to run without getting tired. The soles of his feet no longer wore the pale, fragile skin he had liberated from his shoes. They were covered with a hard crust, the color of the earth. His toes, with their broken nails, had grown farther apart, the better to grip the ground, the stones, the tree trunks.

At first Bony used to make fun of him and his black shoes. He would say, "Fintan pikni!" The other boys laughed with him. Now he could run like them, even on thorns or ant hills.

Bony's village lay across the mouth of the Omerun. The stream water was smooth and transparent, reflecting the sky. Fintan had never seen such a beautiful place. In the village, there were no houses belonging to the English, not even any tin-roofed huts like in Onitsha. The pier was simply made of hardened mud, and the huts had thatched roofs. The pirogues sat drying on the beach, there where the small children played, where the old men repaired their nets and their lines. Upstream there was a beach of gravel and pebbles where the women washed their laundry and themselves, at dusk.

When Fintan arrived there, the women called out insults and threw stones at him. They laughed, they made fun of him in their language. So Bony showed him the way through the reeds at the end of the beach.

The young women were very beautiful—tall and gleaming in the water of the stream. There was a strange woman Bony took him to see each time, through the reeds. The first time he saw her was not long after his arrival, and it was still the rainy season. She was not with the other girls but a little way to one side, bathing in the stream. She had a child's face, very smooth, but her body and breasts were those of a woman. Her hair was knotted in a red scarf, and she wore a cowrie necklace around her throat. The other girls and the children made fun of her; they threw little pips and stones at her. They were afraid of her. She was from nowhere, she had arrived one day on board a pirogue that came from the south, and she had stayed. Her name was Oya. She wore the blue mission dress and a crucifix around her neck. It was said she was a prostitute from Lagos and that she had been in prison. It was said she often went on board the wreck of the English ship moored to the end of Brokkedon Island, in the middle of the river. That is why the girls made fun of her and threw pits at her.

Bony and Fintan often came down to the little beach at the mouth of the Omerun to spy on Oya. It was a wild place with birds, cranes, herons. In the evening the sky turned to yellow and the fields of grass grew dark. Fintan would grow apprehensive. He called to Bony in a low voice. "Come on! Let's leave now!"

Bony was watching for Oya. She was naked in the middle of the stream, washing herself, washing her clothes. Fintan's heart was pounding while he watched her through the reeds. Bony was in front of him, like a cat lying in wait.

Here, in the middle of the water, Oya did not look like the madwoman at whom the children threw pits. She was beautiful. Her body shone in the light, her breasts swollen like those of a real woman. She turned towards them with her smooth face, her long eyes. Perhaps she knew that they were there, hiding in the reeds. She was the black goddess who had crossed the desert, the one who reigned over the river.

One day Bony dared to go up to Oya. When he came onto the beach, the young woman looked at him without fear. She simply took her wet dress to the shore and put it on. Then she slipped in among the reeds, to the path that led back to the town. Bony was with her.

Fintan walked for a moment on the beach. The late afternoon sun was brilliant. Everything was silent and empty; there was only the sound of the stream and, from time to time, a brief note of birdsong. Fintan walked on through the tall grass, his heart pounding. Suddenly he saw Oya. She was lying on the ground and Bony held her as if he were fighting with her. She had thrown her head back, and in her dilated eyes there was fear. She did not cry out; it was just her breathing, rough, like a call without a voice. Suddenly, unaware of what he was doing, Fintan rushed at Bony, striking him with his fist, kicking him, with the anger of a child who seeks to hurt someone bigger. Bony pulled back. His sex was erect. Fintan continued to hit him, so Bony shoved him violently with the palm of his hands. His voice was deep, muted with anger. "Pissop fool, you gughe!"

Oya had slid over the grass, her dress was stained with mud, her face was full of hatred and anger. She suddenly rushed at Fintan and bit his hand, so hard that he cried out in pain. Then she ran off towards the top of the hill.

Fintan went to wash his hand in the stream. Oya's teeth had left a deep mark, in a half circle. The water shone with the brightness of metal; a white haze blurred the treetops. When Fintan turned back, Bony had disappeared.

Fintan ran back to Ibusun. Maou was waiting on the veranda. She was pale and there were rings under her eyes.

"What's the matter, Maou?"

"Where were you?"

"Down by the stream."

He hid the hurt on his hand. He did not want her to know, he was ashamed. It was a secret. Bony must never come to Ibusun.

"I never see you anymore, you're always running off. You know your father does not want you to go around with that Bony boy."

Maou knew Bony. She had seen him on the pier, where he was helping his father to unload the fish. Elijah did not like her. He was a stranger, from the coast, from Degema or Victoria.

Fintan went to his room. He took down his familiar old exercise book and wrote A LONG VOYAGE. Now the black queen was called Oya; she was the one who reigned over the big town on the riverbank, where Esther arrived. For her he wrote in pidgin, inventing a language. He spoke with signs.

Maou lit the oil lamp on the terrace. She looked at the night. She loved the arrival of the storm — it was a deliverance. She waited for the sound of the V8 climbing the steep grade to Ibusun. Fintan came up to her, silently. It was like the day after they first came to Onitsha. They were alone in the night. They held each other very close, their eyes full of lightning, counting the seconds.

Sabine Rodes lived in a sort of castle — made of wood and corrugated iron painted in white — at the other end of town above the old landing pier, in the place where the fishermen pulled up their pirogues to dry upon the muddy beach. The first time Fintan went to his house was with Maou, not long after their arrival. Geoffroy went almost every day to visit him at that time. He went to consult his books and maps for his research. Sabine Rodes had a library with a great many books on the archaeology and anthropology of West Africa, and a collection of objects and masks from Benin, Niger, and even from the Baoulé from the Ivory Coast.

In the beginning Maou had enjoyed visiting Rodes. He was a bit like her, on the fringe of Onitsha's respectable society. Then, abruptly, she began to hate him quite violently, for no reason that Fintan could detect. She stopped going with Geoffroy on his visits and even forbade Fintan from going back there, with no explanation, in the short and definitive tone of voice she adopted when she disliked someone.

Geoffroy continued to go to the white house at the edge of town. There was something too charming about Sabine Rodes; you could not simply stop seeing him, just like that. Fintan also went to the big house, unbeknownst to Maou. He knocked on the big door and went into the garden. That is where he saw Oya again.

Sabine Rodes lived alone in his house, which was an old customs building from the time of the "river consulates." One day he made Fintan come in. He showed him the bullet holes still embedded in the wooden facade, a reminder of the time of the Njawhaw, the "Destroyers." Fintan followed Sabine Rodes, his heart pounding. The big house groaned like the hull of a ship. The frame was being eaten by termites and was patched here and there with pieces of zinc. They entered an immense room with closed shutters; the wooden walls were painted a cream color with a chocolate-colored strip at the base. In the half-light Fintan could just make out a host of extraordinary objects—the dark skins of forest leopards hung on the wall, surrounded by woven leather, sculpted panels, thrones, stools, Baoulé statues with their elongated eyes, Bantu shields, Fang masks, carafes inlaid with pearls, lengths of cloth. An ebony stool was decorated with naked men and women; another was decorated with sexual organs, alternately male and female, sculpted in relief. There was a strange smell of Russian leather, of incense, of sandalwood.

"No one ever comes in here," said Sabine. "Except your father, from time to time, to see his Egyptian gods. And Okawho." Okawho was Rodes's black servant, a silent young man who glided barefoot across the floor. Fintan was astonished by his face, so like the masks in the big dark rooms: an elongated face, with a prominent forehead and slanted eyes. His cheeks and forehead were carved with violet markings. His arms and legs were endless, his fingers long and tapering. "This is my son," said Rodes. "Everything here is his."

When Fintan passed before him, the young man stood to one side, vanishing like a shadow. The white of his eyes shone in the darkness; he melted into the statues.

Sabine Rodes was the strangest man Fintan had ever met. He was without doubt the most despised man in Onitsha's little European community. All sorts of stories made the rounds about him. It was said he had been an actor with the Old Vic in Bristol, that he had joined the army. It was said that he had worked as a spy and still had connections in the Ministry of Defense. At forty-two he was a lean man with an adolescent's bearing, but his hair was already gray. He had a handsome face with regular features and his eyes were a penetrating gray blue; two deep lines on either side of his mouth gave him an expression of irony and good humor, and yet he never laughed.

He was very different from the other Englishmen, and that was, no doubt, what had attracted Geoffroy to him. He was generous, mocking, enthusiastic, and also irascible, cynical, and dishonest. It was said that he had concocted several spectacular hoaxes, going so far as to convince both the Resident and the District Officer that the Prince of Wales was visiting, incognito, on a steamboat down the Niger. He drank whiskey and wine that he obtained from France thanks to Geoffroy. He read a great deal—French theater, even German poets. He refused to dress in the style of the minor civil servants of the colony. He made fun of their too long shorts, their woollen socks, their Cawnpore helmets, and their impeccable black umbrellas. As for Rodes himself, he wore only old canvas trousers, threadbare and full of holes, a Lacoste shirt, and leather sandals, and when he was at home he wore the long, sky blue robe in the style of the Hausas from Kano.

He spoke most of the river languages; he knew Peulh and Arabic. He had no accent in French. When he spoke with Maou he had great fun reciting verses by Manzoni and Alfieri, as if he knew they were her favorites. He had travelled all through West Africa, to the source of the river, to Timbuktu. But he did not talk about it. What pleased him most was to listen to music on his gramophone and go fishing in the river with Okawho.

Maou could not bear for Fintan to continue to visit Sabine Rodes. She had tried to warn Geoffroy, but he did not listen. One day, Fintan heard some strange things. Maou was talking to Geoffroy in her room; her voice was shrill, anxious, her Italian accent suddenly more exaggerated. She spoke about danger, she said things that were difficult to understand about Okawho and Oya, she said he wanted to make them his slaves. She even cried out, "That man is the devil," and that made Geoffroy laugh.

After that discussion, Geoffroy spoke to Fintan. He was about to leave for an appointment at the wharf and he was in a hurry. He told him not to go to Mr. Rodes's house any more. He said, "Rodes is not a very good name, it is not a name like ours. Do you understand?" Fintan didn't understand a thing.

It was grand was to be at the bow of the pirogue when Sabine Rodes went out on the river. Rodes would sit on a little wooden chair in the middle of the pirogue, and Okawho would steer with the outboard motor, a forty-horsepower Evinrude which made a noise like an airplane. At the bow of the pirogue you went faster than sound, and Fintan heard only the wind in his ears and the rushing of water against the prow. Rodes told Fintan to watch out for tree trunks. Sitting forward with his feet brushing across the waves, Fintan took his task very seriously. He would point out the danger spots, waving his arm to the left or the right. When there was a trunk under the surface, he would wave to Okawho to shift the position of the outboard.

Downstream the river grew as wide as the sea. Egrets took flight before the pirogue, along the surface of the gunmetal water, then landed to rest slightly farther away in the reeds. They passed other pirogues laden with yams and plantain, so heavy they seemed on the verge of sinking, and the men had to bail without stopping. Bent over their long poles, the mariners glided along the shore where the current was slowest. Other pirogues, with motors, moved along the middle of the river, in a clamor that resounded like thunder, their sterns listing under the weight of the motor. When Sabine Rodes's pirogue went by, the pilots signalled. But those who were poling their way along remained motionless, impassible. On the river there was no talking. There was only the motion of gliding between the water and the dazzling reflection of the sky.

Then the pirogue turned off into a narrow stream almost sealed by vegetation. Okawho switched off the engine and, standing on the edge of the pirogue, he leaned against the pole. He was slim and his back arched; his scar-streaked face shone in the sun.

The pirogue moved slowly forward among the trees. The forest enclosed the water like a great wall. The silence caused Fintan's heart to pound; it was like entering a cave. There was a cold breath from deep within, powerful, acrid odors. This is where Sabine Rodes came to fish with a harpoon or, on occasion, to chase crocodiles or snakes.

Turning halfway round Fintan saw Rodes standing in the pirogue, just next to him, his spear gun in his hand. There was a strange expression on his face, joy, or perhaps fierceness. He no longer wore his expression of irony or that aloof air of boredom that he affected when speaking with the English inhabitants of Onitsha. There was a hardness in the shine of his gray blue eyes.

"Look!" he whispered, pointing out to Fintan the passage between the branches. The pirogue drifted slowly forward and Okawho crouched down to pass under the vault of vegetation. Fintan looked with horrified fascination at the opaque water. He did not know what he was meant to look at. Dark shapes glided in the water and there were whirlpools. In the deep water lived monsters. Monsters . . . The sun burned through the foliage of the trees.

Sabine Rodes decided to go back. He dropped the gun in the bottom of the pirogue. The day was already over. The rainy season had returned. Black clouds gathered in the sky, downstream, by the sea. There was a sudden growl of thunder and the wind began to blow. Just as the pirogue entered the main river, opposite the island of Jersey, the storm came down upon them. A gray curtain moved along the river, obliterating the riverscape in its passage. Lightning streaked the clouds above them. The wind was so strong that it raised waves on the surface of the water. Sabine Rodes cried out, in Ibo, "Ozoo! Je kanyi la!" Standing at the stern, Okawho steered the motor with one hand, trying to make out the drifting tree trunks. Fintan had curled up in the middle of the pirogue, wrapped in an oilskin that Rodes had given him. There was no time to reach the landing pier in Onitsha. In the half-light, when he turned around, Fintan could see the lights of the wharf, very far away, lost in the liquid immensity. The pirogue was headed towards Jersey Island. Sabine Rodes bailed water with a calabash.

The rain did not reach them immediately. It went in two directions, two arms encircling the island. Okawho seized the chance to run the pirogue right up onto the beach, and Sabine Rodes led Fintan at a run to a hut made of leaves. Then the rain came, with such violence that it tore the leaves from the trees. The wind blew a mist of rain which came into the hut, making it difficult to breathe. It was as if there were no more earth, no river, just this cloud, coming from everywhere, this cold dust penetrating the body.

It lasted for a long time. Fintan crouched down against the wall of the hut. He was cold. Sabine Rodes sat down near him. He had taken off his shirt and wrapped him in it. His gestures were very gentle, fatherly. Fintan felt a great calmness in him.

Sabine Rodes spoke almost in a whisper. He said whatever came into his head. They were alone. Through the opening in the hut the river seemed to have no limits. It was like being on a desert island, in the middle of the ocean.

"You understand me, don't you? You know who I am. You don't hate me like the others, you see perfectly well who I am."

Fintan looked at him. Rodes seemed lost, there was a sort of mist over his eyes, a distress that Fintan did not understand. Fintan thought that he could never hate him, even if he were what Maou said, even if he were the devil.

"They are all leaving, changing. Don't change, pikni, don't ever change, even if everything is falling down around you."

All at once, just as it had come, the rain stopped. The sun came out, a warm yellow light of dusk. When they walked along the shore, Fintan and Sabine Rodes saw the gray cloud disappearing downstream. Brokkedon rose out of the river, the wreck moored to its stern like an enormous animal trapped in the mud.

"Look, pikni. It's the *George Shotton*, it's my ship."

"Is it really yours?" asked Fintan naively.

"It is mine, Oya's, Okawho's—what difference does it make?"

Fintan was cold. He was shivering so terribly that his legs would not support him. Sabine Rodes took him on his back and carried him to the pirogue, where Okawho stood waiting, his body glistening with raindrops. On his face was an expression of wild joy. Sabine Rodes settled Fintan, still wrapped in his old shirt, in the wooden armchair.

Je kanyi la! The bow of the pirogue pointed towards the pier at Onitsha. The hull slapped through the waves, and the airplane roar of the outboard filled the entire visible expanse of river, from one shore to the other.

As evening fell, there was always a moment of peace, of emptiness. Fintan went to the fishermen's quay, to wait. He knew that Bony had already gone up the dusty road where the chained convicts would pass by.

The river flowed gently, with knotlike gurgles, whirlpools, little sucking noises. Sabine Rodes said it was the biggest river in the world, because in its flow it carried the entire history of mankind since the beginning. In Geoffroy's office Fintan had seen a big drawing pinned to the wall, a map representing the Nile and the Niger. At the top of the map was written PTOLÉMAÏS and, everywhere, strange names, Ammon, Lac de Lyconède, Garamantiké, Pharax, Melanogaitouloï, Geïra, Nigeira Metropolis. Between the rivers a line drawn in red pencil marked the route taken by the queen of Meroë when she set off to find another world with all her people.

Fintan looked at the opposite shore, so far away in the declining light that it seemed unreal, just like the coast of Africa from the deck of the *Surabaya*. The islands floated above the sparkling water. Jersey, Brokkedon, and the nameless shoals where logs were trapped. At the tip of Brokkedon was the wreck of the *George Shotton*, half-sunken, covered with trees, like the carcass of some hairy giant. Sabine Rodes had promised to take Fintan to the wreck, but he was not to mention it to anyone.

So Fintan came down to watch the river, to wait for the arrival of the pirogues. There was something terrible and reassuring at the same time about the flowing movement of the water, something that caused your heart to beat faster, that burned your eyes. In the evening, when he could not sleep, Fintan would pick up his old exercise book and continue to write the story A LONG JOURNEY: Esther's boat heading upriver, as big as a floating city, all the inhabitants of Meroë on board. Esther was the queen: with her they travelled towards the country with such a fine name, the name Fintan had read on the map pinned to the wall: GAO.

On the dusty road, Bony was waiting. Every evening at six o'clock, when the sun dropped down on the other side of the river, the convicts would leave D.O. Simpson's property to go back to the prison in town. Bony watched for their arrival, half hidden by the fence that surrounded the property. There were other people on the dusty road, mainly women, children. They had brought food and cigarettes. It was the time when they could give packets and letters or simply call out to the prisoners, say their names.

First of all came the sound of the chain moving forward in fits and starts; then the voices of the policemen, chanting the rhythm of their steps: "One! One!" If a convict fell out of step, the weight of the chain would trip his left leg and throw him to the ground.

Fintan had joined Bony at the edge of the road just as the little group arrived. The ragged prisoners walked quickly, one behind the other, carrying a shovel or a pick on their shoulders. Their faces shone with sweat; their bodies were dusted with red powder.

On either side of the prisoners policemen in khaki uniforms, Cawnpore helmets, and sturdy, black shoes walked in step with the convicts, rifles on their shoulders. The women at the roadside called out to the prisoners and ran forward to try to give them what they had brought, but the policemen pushed them away: "Go away! Pissop fool!"

In the middle of the small group was a tall thin man, his face marked by fatigue. As he went by, his eyes paused for a moment upon Bony, then on Fintan. Such a strange look, empty and at the same time full of meaning. Bony merely said, "Ogbo," because it was his uncle. The prisoners marched past them, stepping in time, heading down the dusty road towards the town. The light of the setting sun touched the treetops, caused the sweat on the convicts' skin to glow. The scraping of the long chain seemed to tear something from the earth. Then the prisoners entered the town, followed by the gaggle of women who continued to cry out the prisoners' names. Bony went back to the river. He did not speak. Fintan went with him as far as the quay to watch the slow movement of the water. He did not want to go back to Ibusun. He wanted to leave, set off on a pirogue, and glide away, anywhere, as if the earth had ceased to exist.

Maou opened her eyes onto the night. She listened to the night noises, the creaking of the house, the wind blowing dust onto the tin roof. The wind came from the desert, burning people's faces. The room was red. Maou pushed aside the mosquito net. The plank wall was lit by a Punkah lamp; moths clustered impatiently around the lamp's halo. At times the chirring of the crickets rose, then fell again. Now and again, too, Mollie's furtive, hunting step, and the cries of feral cats burning with love for her on the tin roofs.

Geoffroy was not there. What time could it possibly be? She had fallen asleep without dinner, reading *The African Witch* by Joyce Cary. Fintan had not come back yet. She waited for him on the veranda, then went to bed. She had a fever.

Maou shuddered suddenly. She heard the beating of drums, far away, on the other side of the river, like breathing. It was this sound which had awoken her, without her realizing, like a shiver on her skin.

She wanted to find out the time, but her wristwatch was still on the small table next to the night light. Her book had fallen to the ground. She could not remember what it was about. She remembered that her eyelids had been closing all by themselves, that the lines of text became muddled. She had to read the same sentence several times over, and it was different each time.

Now she was wide awake. In the lamplight she could make out

every detail, every shadow, every object, on the table, on the trunk, on the planks of the wall, on the rust-spotted canvas of the false ceiling. She could not tear her gaze away from those spots, those shadows; it was as if she were seeking to solve a puzzle.

The distant beating stopped, then began again. A breathing. It also meant something, but what? Maou did not understand. She could think of nothing, nothing but loneliness, the night, the heat, the noise of insects.

She wanted to get up, to go and drink something. She didn't care about the time anymore. She walked barefoot through the house, to the earthenware drinking filter in the pantry. She waited for the pewter cup to fill. She drank the tasteless water in one gulp.

The drumbeats had ceased. She was no longer even sure she had heard them. Perhaps it was nothing but the grumbling of the storm, far away, or else the throbbing of her own blood in her arteries. She walked barefoot across the floor, trying to sense the presence of scorpions or cockroaches in the near darkness. Her heart was pounding; she felt a shiver at the base of her neck, down her back. She went into every room in the house. Fintan's room was empty. The mosquito net was in place. Maou went on to Geoffroy's office. For some time now Geoffroy had no longer been coming into his office to write in his notebooks. On the table were books and papers in an untidy heap. Maou shone the light of an electric torch on the table. To control her anxiety she feigned interest in the books and newspapers, the crumpled copies of the *African Advertiser*, the *West African Star*, an issue of *War Cry*, a newsletter from the Salvation Army. On a board supported by two bricks there were law books and the *Directory of the Commercial Ports of the West*. There were other bound books, spoiled by humidity, that Geoffroy had bought in London. Maou read the names out loud: *Talk Boy* by Margaret Mead, which Geoffroy had given her to read when she first arrived, and *Black Byzantium* by Siegfried Nadel. Several volumes by E. A. Wallis Budge, *Osiris and the Egyptian Resurrection*, *The Chapter of the Coming Forth*, and *From Fetish to God*. Novels, too, which she had begun to read, *Mr. Johnson* and *Sanders of the River* by Joyce Cary, *Plain Tales from the Hills* by Rudyard Kipling, travel stories, Percy Amaury Talbot, C. K. Meek, and *Loose Among the Devils* by Sinclair Gordon.

She went out on the veranda and was astonished by the softness of the night. The strong light of the full moon. Through the foliage of the trees, far away, she saw the great river, shining like the sea.

That is why she was shivering, because of the night, so beautiful, this silver blue moonlight, this silence rising from the earth, merging with the beating of her heart. She wanted to speak, she wanted to cry out, "Fintan! Where are you?"

But her throat caught. She could make no sound.

She went back into the house and shut the door. In Geoffroy's office she had lit the lamp, and already butterflies and flying ants burned on the light, sizzling. In the drawing room she lit other lamps. The African armchairs made of red wood were terrifying. Emptiness was everywhere, on the big table, on the glass cabinets containing glasses and enamelled plates.

"Fintan! Where are you?" Maou circled through the rooms, lighting the lamps one after the other. Now the entire house was lit up, as if for a party. The lamps heated the air, there was an odor of paraffin so you could scarcely breathe. Maou sat under the veranda on the floor with a lamp propped next to her. The cool breeze caused the flame to flicker. The insects burst in from the deep night, knocking against the walls; their whirling dance around the lamps made one think of madness. Maou felt her cotton shirt sticking to her skin, cool drops tickling her sides, under her armpits.

Suddenly she began to walk. As fast as she could, her bare feet beating against the laterite road which led to town. She ran to the river, along the road illuminated by moonlight. She heard the sound of her heartbeat — or was it the beat of hidden drums on the other side of the river? The wind wrapped her shirt around her belly, against her chest, and she felt the hard, cool earth beneath her feet, resonant like a living skin.

She arrived in the town. Electric lamps shone outside the customs buildings, by the hospital. On the wharf there was a row of street lamps. People stepped aside as she moved forward. She heard shouts, whistles. Dogs howled at her passage. There were women dressed in long, multicolored dresses sitting on their doorsteps, laughing raucously.

Maou did not really know where she was going. She saw the company warehouses but apart from the lights shining above the doors everything was dark and closed. Slightly higher up, in the middle of a garden surrounded by a fence, was the Resident's house. She continued walking, as far as the D.O.'s house, to the Club. There she stopped and, without even pausing to catch her breath, she began tapping on the door, calling. Just behind the Club was the gaping hole of the future swimming pool, full of muddy water. In the electric light you could see things floating, turds, perhaps, or even rats.

Then, before the doors and windows were even opened, before the Club members appeared with their drinks in their hands and their powdered faces which made her want to laugh through her tears, Maou felt her legs give way, as if someone, a hidden dwarf, had tripped her. She collapsed upon herself in a heap, her hands pressed against her chest, her breath locked in her body, trembling from head to foot.

"Maria Luisa, Maria Luisa . . ."

Geoffroy took her in his arms, carried her like a child to the car. "What is wrong, you're not well, speak to me." His voice was strange, somewhat hoarse. He smelled of alcohol. Maou heard other voices, Rally's reedy tones, Gerald Simpson's sarcastic accent. Rally said, repeatedly, "If there is anything I can do . . ." As the car sped along the road, piercing the night with its headlamps, Maou felt that everything was coming undone inside her. She said, "Fintan's not at home, I'm so afraid . . ." At the same time she thought she should not have said that, because Geoffroy would hit Fintan with his cane, as he did each time he got angry. She said, "He must have got too hot, he went for a walk. You see, I was all alone in that house."

Elijah was there, in front of the brightly lit house. Geoffroy went with Maou to her room and laid her on the bed under the mosquito net. "Sleep, Maria Luisa. Fintan is back." Maou said, "You won't beat him?"

Geoffroy went out. She heard a burst of voices. Then nothing more. Geoffroy came to sit on the edge of the bed, the upper part of his body inside the mosquito net.

"He was at the quay. It was Elijah who brought him home."

Maou felt like laughing. At the same time she felt her eyes fill with tears. Geoffroy left to turn off all the lights, one after the other. Then he came back and lay down in the bed. Maou was cold. She put her arms around Geoffroy's body.

She wanted to find Geoffroy's words again, everything he had said in those days. It was before their marriage, so long ago. There was no war, no ghetto in Saint-Martin, no escape through the mountains to Santa Anna. Everything was so young at that time, so innocent. In San Remo, the little room with the green shutters, the afternoon with the cooing of turtledoves in the garden, the shimmering of the sea. They would make love, slowly and gently; it was luminous like the blaze of the sun. There was no need for words at that time; or else Geoffroy would wake her up sometimes, in the night, to speak a few words of English to her. "I am so fond of you, Marilu." It had become their song. He wanted her to speak in Italian, to sing, but she knew nothing other than Grandmother Aurelia's nursery rhymes.

> Ninna nanna ninna-o!
> Questo bimbo a chi lo do?
> Lo daro alla Befana
> che lo tiene una settimana.
> Lo daro all'uomo Nero
> che lo tiene un mese intero!

In the evening they would go to bathe in the warm sea, smooth as a lake, among the rocks crusted with violet sea urchins. They would swim together, very slowly, to see the sun dropping behind the hills, setting the greenhouses alight with flame. The sea became the color of the sky, impalpable, unreal. One day he said, because he was leaving for Africa, "Out there, people believe that a child is born the day he is created, and that he belongs to the earth where he was conceived." She remembered that that had caused her to shudder, because she already knew that she was expecting a baby, had known since the beginning of summer. But she hadn't told him. She didn't want him to worry or abandon his journey. They were married at the end of the summer, and Geoffroy set sail for Africa immediately afterwards. Fintan was born in March 1936, in a dilapidated clinic in Nice's old town. At that time Maou wrote to Geoffroy, a long letter telling him everything, but she did not receive a reply until three months later, because of the strikes. Time had gone by. Fintan was too small, Aurelia would never have allowed them to leave, to go so far, for such a long time. Geoffroy came back in the summer of 1939. They took the train to San Remo, as if it were still the same summer, the same room with the green shutters closed against the sparkling of the sea. Fintan slept next to them in his small bed. They dreamt of another life, in Africa. Maou would have liked Canada, Vancouver Island. Then Geoffroy left again, a few days before war was declared. It was too late, there were no more letters. When Italy declared war in June 1940, they had to flee, with Aurelia and Rosa, to hide in the mountains above Saint-Martin; they had to have false papers made, false names. It all seemed so far away now. Maou recalled the taste of tears, such long days, such loneliness.

Geoffroy's breath burned the nape of her neck, she could feel her heartbeat. Or was it the drumbeats in the night, on the far shore of the river? But she was no longer afraid. "I love you." She heard his voice, his breathing. "I am so fond of you, Marilu." He tightened his arms around her; she felt a wave rising within, the way it had once been, when everything was new. "Nothing has happened, I've never left you." The wave inside her grew bigger, going through Geoffroy's body too. The deep, continuous swell was one with the wave, carrying them on the river as it had carried them on the sea, then, in Italy; it was an intoxicating sound, a calming sound, it was the sound of the storm dying on a different shore.

The *harmattan* was blowing. The hot wind had dried the sky and the earth, and there were wrinkles on the mud of the river like the skin of a very old animal. The river was an azure blue, there were immense beaches full of birds. The steamboat no longer went as far as Onitsha; it stopped to unload the merchandise at Degema. At the tip of Brokke-don Island the *George Shotton* lay in the silt, just like the carcass of a sea monster.

During the day Geoffroy no longer went to the wharf. The offices of the United Africa were veritable furnaces because of the tin roofs. He would go down towards evening to fetch the mail, check the account books, the transfer of merchandise. Then he would go to the Club, but he found it more and more difficult to tolerate the atmosphere there. D.O. Simpson would be telling his never ceasing safari stories, his drink in his hand. Since the incident with Maou he had become insolent, sarcastic, hateful. There had been no progress with the pool. The sides had not been shored up properly and one of them had collapsed, injuring the convicts. Geoffroy had come home indignant: "That bastard, he could have removed their chain to let them work!"

Maou was on the verge of tears. "How can you go to see him, how can you go into his house?"

"I shall speak to the Resident, this can't go on."

But Geoffroy forgot. He would lock himself in his room, behind his desk, where he had pinned Ptolemy's big map. He was reading, taking notes, checking maps.

One afternoon Fintan stood in the doorway. He was looking in, timidly, and his father called to him; Geoffroy seemed distracted, his gray hair was untidy, the bald patch on his crown was visible. Fintan tried to think of him as his father. It was not very easy.

"You know, boy, I think I have the key to the problem." He spoke with a certain vehemence. He pointed to the map pinned on the wall. "Ptolemy explains everything. The Jupiter Ammon oasis is too far north, impossible. The proper way is by way of Kufra, through the Ethiopian mountains, then down to the south, because of Girgiri, as far as the swamps of the Chilonides, or even further south, towards the Nuba country. The Nuba were allies of the last inhabitants of Meroë. From there, following the underground flow of the river, at night, they found all the water they needed, by capillary action, for themselves and for their cattle. And one day, years later, they must have come upon the big river, the new Nile."

He spoke as he walked, removing then replacing his eyeglasses. Fintan was a little bit frightened, and at the same time he listened to the pieces of this extraordinary story — the names of mountains, of wells in the desert.

"Meroë: the city of the black queen, the last representative of Osiris, the last descendant of the Pharaohs. Kemit, the black country. In 350 Meroë was sacked by King Ezana of Axum. He entered the city with his troops, mercenaries from the Nuba country, and all the people of Meroë, the scribes, the scholars, the architects, went away, taking their herds and their sacred treasures; they walked behind the queen, searching for a new world. . . ."

He spoke as if it were his own story, as if he had arrived there, at the end of his journey, by the River Geir, in that mysterious town which had become the new Meroë, as if the river that flowed past Onitsha were the way to the other side of the world, towards Hesperiou Keras, the Horn of the West, towards Theon Ochema, the Chariot of the Gods, towards the guardian peoples of the forest.

Fintan listened to all these names, he listened to the voice of this man who was his father, and he felt tears in his eyes, without understanding why. Perhaps it was because of the sound of his voice, so stifled, as if he was not really addressing Fintan but was speaking to himself alone—or was it because of what he was saying, the dream which came from such a great distance, those names in an unfamiliar language which he read hastily from a map pinned to the wall, as if a moment later it would be too late, as if everything would escape: Garamantes, Thoumelitha, Panagra, Tayama, and the name written in red capital letters, NIGEIRA METROPOLIS, at the confluence of the rivers, at the edge of the desert and the forest, there where the world had begun again. The city of the black queen.

It was hot. Flying ants circled the lamps, the moths hung in the patches of light, their heads with their motionless eyes at the center of a halo of mosquitoes.

Fintan was still on the doorstep. He observed this feverish man pacing back and forth in front of his map; he listened to his voice. He tried to imagine the city, in the middle of the river, that mysterious city where time had stood still. But what he saw was Onitsha, motionless at the edge of the river, with its dusty streets and its houses with their rusty tin roofs, the piers, the United Africa buildings, Sabine Rodes's mansion, and the gaping hole in front of Gerald Simpson's house. Perhaps it was too late already.

"Go now, leave me alone."

Geoffroy sat down behind his table heaped with papers. He looked tired. Fintan backed away noiselessly.

"Close the door."

He had a way of saying "the doh-aw" in his funny accent that made Fintan think he might be able to love him, despite his nasty temper, his violence. Fintan closed the door, releasing the knob very gently, as if he were afraid of waking him. And at once he felt a tightening in his throat and tears in his eyes. He went to find Maou in her room and huddled up against her. He was afraid of what was going to happen, he would have preferred never to have come here, to Onitsha. "Speak to me in your language." She sang a nursery rhyme, just like in the old days.

The first lines of the tattoo are the emblem of the sun, the Itsi Ngweri, the sons of Eri, the first of the Umundri, the lineage of the Edze Ndri. Moises, who speaks all the languages of the bay of Biafra, says to Geoffroy:

"The people of Agbaja call the signs tattooed on the cheeks of young men Ogo, that is, the wings and the tail of the falcon. But all of them call God Chuku, that is, the Sun."

He speaks of the god who sends rain and harvests. He says, "He is every-where, he is the spirit of the sky."

Geoffroy writes these words, then he repeats the words of the Egyptian *Book of the Dead*, where it is said:

I am the God Shu, my seat is in the eye of the father.

Moises speaks of the "chi," of the soul, he speaks of the Anyangu, Lord of the Sun, for whom blood sacrifices were made. Moises says: "When I was still a child, the people of Awka were called the Sons of the Sun, because they were faithful to our god."

He says, "The Jukun, on the banks of the river Benue, call the sun Anu."

Geoffroy shudders as he hears this name, because he remembers the words of the *Book of the Dead* and the name of the king of Heliopolis: Iunu, the Sun.

There is an exhilaration. The truth burns, dazzles. The world is but a passing shadow, a veil through which the oldest names of creation appear. In the north, the people of Adamawa call the sun Anyara, the son of Ra. The Ibos of the south say Anyanu, the eye of Anu, which the Bible calls On.

The words of the *Book of the Dead* vibrate with force, are still alive, here, in Onitsha, on the banks of the river:

The city of Anu is like him, Osiris, a god.
Anu is like him, a god. Anu is as he is, Ra.
Anu is as he is, Ra. His mother is Anu.
His father is Anu, he himself is Anu, born in Anu.

Knowledge is infinite. The river has never ceased to flow between these same shores. Its water is the same. Now Geoffroy watches with his eyes as it flows downstream, the heavy water laden with the blood of men, the river which eviscerates the earth, devours the forest.

He walks along the quay, beside the deserted buildings. The sun sparkles on the surface of the river. He is looking for men whose faces are marked with the sign of the Itsi. Along the water glide pirogues and drifting tree trunks, with their branches plunging like animal arms.

"In the past," says Moises, "the chiefs of the tribe in Benin were jealous of the Oba, and decided to seek revenge on his only son called Ginuwa. The Oba, once he understood that after his death his son would be assassinated by the chiefs of the tribe, had a great chest made. In the chest he locked away seventy-two children from the families of the chiefs of the tribes, and he made his own son go into the chest, carrying food and a magic wand. Then he had the chest carried to the water at the mouth of the river, that it might set sail towards the sea. The chest floated upon the water for days, until it reached a town called Ugharegi, near the town of Sapele. There, the chest opened, and Ginuwa stepped out on the shore, followed by the seventy-two children."

100

There is only one legend, one river. Set, the enemy, helped by seventy-two accomplices, locks Osiris in a chest made in his image and seals the chest with molten lead. Then he throws the chest into the Nile, that it be carried to the Delta and to the sea. And so Osiris rises above death and becomes God.

Geoffroy grows dizzy with watching the river. In the evening, when the Umundri return in their long pirogues, he walks up to them and repeats the ritual greeting, like the words of a magic formula, the ancient words of Ginuwa:

"*Ka ts'i so, ka ts'i so* . . . Until the sun does rise again . . ."

He wants to receive the *chi,* he wants to be like them, one with eternal knowledge, one with the oldest path in the world. One with the river and the sky, one with Anyanu, with Inu, with Igwe, one with the father of Ale, with the earth, with the father of Amodi Oha, the lightning, to be one face, with the sign of eternity etched into the skin in copper dust: Ongwa, the moon, Anyanu, the sun, and on either side of the cheeks Odudu Egbe, the plumes of the wings and tail of the falcon. In this way:

Geoffroy walks back along the endless road.

She is the one he sees, now, in a dream; she is the black queen, the last queen of Meroë, fleeing the ruins of the town pillaged by Axum's soldiers. She is there, surrounded by the crowd of her people, notables and ministers, scholars and architects, but also peasants and fishermen, blacksmiths, musicians, weavers, potters. Surrounded by the children carrying baskets of food, leading herds of goats, cows with big almond eyes, whose lyre-shaped horns carry the disc of the sun.

She is alone before the crowd, the only one to know her destiny. What is the name of this last queen of Meroë, the queen whom the men of the north have chased from her realm, propelling her into the greatest adventure on earth?

She is the one he wishes to see, now—Candace, perhaps, like the black queen of Meroë—one-eyed and strong as a man, leading her troops against Caesar, conquering the Elephantine Island. That is what Strabon called her, but her true name was Amanirenas.

Four hundred years later, the young queen knows she will never again see the water of the great river, that the sun will never rise again above the tombs of the ancient kings of Meroë: Kashta, Shabako, Shebitku, Taharqa, Anlamani, Karkamani. There will be no more books in which to write the names of queens: Bartare, Shanakdakhete, Lakhideamani . . . Her son may also be called Sharkarer, like the king who defeated the Egyptian army at Jebel Qeili.

But the one he sees is not a ceremonial queen, carried upon her palanquin under a plumed canopy, surrounded by priests and musicians. It is an emaciated woman wrapped in a white veil, barefoot in the desert sand in the midst of a famished horde. Her hair hangs loose upon her shoulders, the light of the sun burns her face, her arms, her chest. On her forehead she still wears the golden circle of Osiris, Khenti Amenti, the Lord of Abydos, from Busiris, and the diadem on which are carved the signs of the sun and the moon, and the plumes of the falcon's wings. Around her neck she wears the head of Maat, the father of the gods, the ram with a scarab's antennae tightly clasping Ankh, the drawing of life, and Usr, the word of strength, in this way:

$$\left\{ \begin{array}{c} \varphi \\ \top \end{array} \right\}$$

She has been walking already for days with her people, opening the route that leads to the place where the sun disappears each evening, Ateb, the entry to the tunnel on the western shore of the celestial river. She is walking with her people in the most terrible desert, the place where the burning wind blows, where the horizon is but a lake of fire, the place where only scorpions and vipers dwell, where fever and death lurk at night between the walls of the tents, stealing the breath of old men and children.

When the day of departure arrives, the black queen gathers her people on the square at Kasu before the smoking ruins of the temples torched by the warriors from Himyar, the soldiers of Axum, of Atbara. The high priests of God, their heads shaved and their feet bare as a sign of mourning, are crouched down on the square. In their hands they hold the insignia of power and the eternal strength of heaven: bronze mirrors and sacred stones. In a wooden box all the books are locked away, the book of the dead, the book of breathing, the book of the resurrection and the judgment. It is before dawn, when the sky is still darker than the earth.

Then when the sun appears, lighting the expanse of the river and the beaches where the rafts lie ready, for the last time in Meroë the prayer rings out, and all the men and women of the people turn towards the resplendent disc as it bursts from the earth, carried by the invisible Ankh:

"O disc, lord of the earth, who has made all beings of the sky and the earth, who has made the world and the ocean depths, who brings into existence men and women, o disc, life and force, beauty, we salute you!"

The voices of the high priests have ceased to echo amidst the silence of the ruins. And so begins the slow noise of departure, the women who call out to gather their animals, the crying of children, the calls of the men pushing the reed rafts towards the middle of the river.

Enemy armies wait everywhere, ready to wreak their vengeance upon the last inhabitants of Kasu, the sons of Aton, the last priests of the sun. To the south and the east, the red warriors, the soldiers of the king Aganes, have come from the mountains of Ethiopia, from the distant city of Axum.

Men and women from Meroë have already begun to head southward, following the river upstream to find a new land. It is said they went as far as the place where the river divides, an arm to the south, towards the Mountains of the Moon, an arm to the east, and that they sailed along that arm to a place called Alwa. Who knows what became of them?

But now it is too late. The warriors of Axum have cut off the route to the south, the Ethiopians occupy the right bank. And then one night the black queen was visited by a dream. In her dream she saw another land, another realm, so far away that no man could reach it in his lifetime, so far away that only the children would be able to see it. A realm beyond the desert and the mountains, a realm very near the roots of the world, there where the sun ends its passage, at the place where the tunnel through the abysses opens out on the domain of Tuat, beneath the universe of men.

She saw it clearly, because it was a dream sent to her by Ra, the lord of

104

eternal life. In that other world on the other side of the desert there is a great river, just like the River Nile, flowing to the south. On its banks stretch immense forests inhabited by ferocious beasts. Then there begin the fertile plains, the savannah where herds of buffalo, elephant, and rhinoceros roam, where lions roar. In that place there is a river like a boundless sea, there are beaches, islands, countless estuaries, reeds where birds and crocodiles live. On an island in the middle of the river the queen saw her new realm, the new city where her people would settle, the sons of Aton, the last inhabitants of Kasu, of Meroë. She saw the city, with all its temples, houses, and busy squares, in the nameless island in the middle of the river. And that is how she decided to leave with the people of Meroë.

All night they gathered before the ruins and the tombs, vigilant, ready to wage the ultimate battle. They enclosed the herds in circles of stones. The men prepared the tents and sacks of wheat; they prepared the weapons and the tools. The animals they could not take with them were sacrificed, and during the night the women smoked the meat. Before the end of the night everything was ready. The men set fire to their own homes, so that what remained would be reduced to ashes and of no use to the enemy. No one slept that night.

At dawn, in the square of Kasu, they prayed and received the blessing of Aton, who is setting out to sail along the river of the sky. Now the reed rafts depart the shore, one after the other, silently. They are so numerous that they make a moving road across the river.

For nine days the rafts glide along the shore towards the setting sun, to the great bend where the river begins its descent to the north. At the foot of the cliff the people gather with their cattle and their provisions.

At dawn on the tenth day they receive the blessing of the winged disc. The women load the baskets on their shoulders, the children gather the herds, and they begin to walk along the endless road towards the Manu mountains where the sun is said to disappear every evening.

As she leaves the shore of the river, about to go deep into the hills of stones, the queen looks one last time behind her. But there are no more tears in her eyes. She feels a great emptiness deep within, because she knows that she will never see the river again, and that her daughter, and the daughter of her daughter, will never see it again. Slowly, the winged disc climbs into the sky. Its invulnerable gaze lights up the world. The queen has begun to walk barefoot over the scorched earth; she follows her silent people on the invisible path of her dream.

"Look, pikni. Allow me to introduce *George Shotton*, in person." Sabine Rodes's pirogue drew near the black wreck wallowing in the mud at the tip of Brokkedon Island. Its bow struck the waves on the river. At the stern stood Okawho, one foot pressed against the handle of the outboard motor, his face shining with scars. Oya was next to him. Just before they left, she came onto the dock, and Sabine Rodes waved to her to climb on board. Now she looked straight ahead, indifferently.

But Sabine Rodes wore an expression of strange jubilation. He spoke loudly, in his theatrical voice.

"*George Shotton*, pikni. Now it's nothing but an old rotten carcass, but it wasn't always like that. She was the biggest hull on the river before the war. Pride of the Empire. Armored like a battleship, with paddle wheels—she used to go up the river to the north, to Yola, Borgawa, Bussa, Gungawa." He pronounced the names slowly, as if he wanted Fintan to remember them forever. The wind ruffled his hair with its white streaks; the light accentuated the wrinkles on his face, the blueness of his eyes. There was no longer anything cruel about the way he looked at you, only amusement.

The bow of the pirogue was headed straight for the hull. The roar of the engine spanned the river, frightening the herons hidden in the reeds. Fintan could clearly make out trees at the top of the wreck that had taken root on deck, inside the hatches.

"Look, pikni, *George Shotton* was the most powerful boat of the Empire here on the river, with her machine guns. Can you see, can you see how she used to go upriver—the savages would dance, the sorcerers with their jujus, so that this enormous animal would go back to where it had come from, to the depths of the ocean!"

He rattled on, standing in the middle of the pirogue. Now Okawho had stopped the engine, for the water was no longer deep enough. They were near the bottom, gliding among the reeds, in the shadow of the immense hulk encrusted with barnacles.

"Look, pikni! Here, in this hull, the officers would stand to attention when Sir Frederick Lugard came on board with his great plumed hat! With him came the kings of Calabar, Owerri, Kabba, Onitsha, Ilorin, with their wives and their slaves. Chukuani of Udi . . . Onuoorah from Nnawi . . . the Obi of Otolo, the old Nuosu wearing his leopard skin . . . the warlords of Ohafia . . . even the envoys of the Obi of Benin, even Jaja, the old fox Jaja from Opobo, who had resisted the English for so long. . . . They all came on board the *George Shotton* to sign their peace treaties."

The pirogue continued under its own momentum, at a slight angle, into the middle of the reeds. There was only the sound of water flowing, the cries of egrets, far away, the waves sucking chunks of mud away from the shore. The black hulk lay before them, keeled over to one side, a massive rusting wall to which the grasses clung. To allay their fears, perhaps, Sabine Rodes continued to speak, snatches of sentences, while the pirogue drifted along the hull. "Look, pikni, she was the finest boat on the river, she carried supplies, weapons, Nordenfelt cannons on their tripods, as well as officers, medical supplies, local people. She used to anchor here, in the middle of the river, and the launches would come and go to the shore, unloading goods. . . . She was known as the Consulate of the River. Now, look, trees have grown inside her. . . ."

From time to time, the bow of the pirogue knocked against the hull here and there, causing the great, empty hull to reverberate. Water lapped against the rusted steel. There were clouds of mosquitoes. At the top of the hull, where the fo'c'sle used to be, trees now grew, as if on an island.

Oya was standing now, too, a statue of black stone. Her mission dress clung to her body with sweat. Fintan looked at her smooth face, her disdainful mouth, her eyes slanted towards her temples. The crucifix sparkled on her chest. He thought that she must be the one, the princess of the ancient realm, the one whose name Geoffroy was searching for. She had come back to the river to look upon the ruin of those who had defeated her people.

For the first time Fintan felt deep within what bound Okawho and Oya to the river. It made his heart beat violently, with dread and impatience. He no longer listened to what Sabine Rodes was saying. Standing at the bow of the pirogue, he looked into the water, the reeds parting before them, the shadow of the hull.

The pirogue stopped against the side of the wreck. There was a metal ladder there, half torn away. Oya jumped up first, followed by Okawho, who tied up the pirogue. Fintan took hold of the guardrail and pulled himself up on the ladder.

The metal rungs moved under his feet, echoing strangely against the silence of the wreck. Oya was already at the top of the ladder, running on the deck through the undergrowth. She seemed to know the way.

Fintan stayed on the deck, clinging to the guardrail. Okawho had disappeared into the depths of the wreck. The deck was laid with wooden planks, most of them broken or rotten. The incline was so steep that Fintan had to crawl on his hands and knees to move around.

The wreck was immense and empty. Here and there you could see remnants of what had been the poop deck, the fo'c'sle, the stumps of the masts. There was nothing left of the aftercastle but a mass of metal. Trees had grown through the portholes.

A hatch was open onto the ruins of a baroque stairway. Sabine Rodes went down the stairway, following Oya and Okawho. Fintan, too, went down into the hull.

Craning his neck, he tried to make out what was ahead of him, but he was dazzled as if this were the entry to a cave. The stairway spiralled down to a huge room invaded by creepers and dead branches. The air was stifling, oppressive with insects. Fintan looked around without daring to move. He thought he saw the metallic flash of a snake. He shivered.

The noise of their breathing filled the room. Near a blocked window through which daylight filtered Fintan could see a broken bulkhead and the interior of an ancient bathroom, where a turquoise green bathtub reigned. On the wall there was a large oval mirror, which lit the room like a window. Then he saw them, Oya and Okawho, on the floor of the bathroom. There was only the sound of their breathing, rapid, difficult. Oya lay on her back on the ground, and Okawho was holding her, as if he were hurting her. In the darkness Fintan could see Oya's face, with a strange expression, an emptiness. As if her eyes were veiled, blinkered.

Fintan shuddered. Sabine Rodes was there, too, hiding in the shadow. His eyes were fixed upon the couple, as if he could not look away, and his lips were murmuring incomprehensible things. Fintan stepped back, looking for the stairway, to go away. His heart was throbbing, and he felt frightened.

Suddenly there was a terrible noise, a thunderclap. Turning around, Fintan saw Okawho standing in the half-light with a weapon in his hand. Then he understood that with a length of pipe Okawho had just broken the big mirror. Oya was next to him, standing against the wall.

110

A smile lit her face. There was something in her of the wild warrior. She let out a hoarse yell which echoed throught the hull. Sabine Rodes took Fintan by the arm and made him step back.

"Come, pikni. Don't look at her. She's mad."

They went back up the staircase. Okawho stayed below, with her. After many minutes he came up. His scar-streaked face was like a mask; one could read nothing there. He also looked like a warrior.

When they were in the pirogue, Okawho cast off. Oya appeared on the deck in the middle of the undergrowth. The pirogue moved slowly along the hull, as if to leave without her. With an animal vitality Oya let herself down, clinging to the creepers and the rough patches on the hull, then jumped into the pirogue just as Okawho was pulling on the ignition cord. The noise of the engine filled the river, echoed inside the empty hull.

The water boiled around the propeller. The pirogue sliced through the reeds. In a moment they were in the middle of the river. Water splashed on either side of the hull, wind filled their ears. Oya stood at the bow of the pirogue, holding her arms slightly outstretched, her body shining with beads of water and her goddesslike face turned slightly to the side, to watch the deepest place of the river.

They reached Onitsha as night fell.

And now it is all no more than a dream dreamt by Geoffroy Allen, in the night, next to Maou sleeping. The town is a raft on the river, where the oldest memory of the world is flowing. That is the city he wants to see now. He feels that if he could just reach that city something would cease in the inhuman movement, in the slipping of the world towards death. As if man's maneuverings could alter the course of the world's oscillations, and the remnants of lost civilizations would emerge from the earth, bursting forth with their secrets and their power, to engender eternal light.

This movement, the slow march of the people of Meroë, year after year towards the setting sun, along the earth's crevices in search of water, the sound of the wind in the palm leaves, in search of the radiant body of the river.

Now he sees her, the old woman, emaciated, faltering, who can no longer step with her blue, swollen feet upon the ground, who must be carried on a stretcher, sheltered from the sun by a length of torn cloth which a child carries on the end of a stick like some pathetic emblem.

Over her almond-shaped eyes, which were once so beautiful, there is a white veil, through which she can see only the change between day and night. This is why the aged queen does not give the signal for departure until the sun has reached its zenith and begun its descent towards the entrance to the world of the dead.

The people follow their invisible path. At times the priests break into a song of sadness and death, a song she can no longer hear, as if a wall has already separated her from the living. The black queen leans over on her stretcher, which swings to the rhythm of her warriors' shoulders. Before her, through her veiled eyes, shines the distant light she can never reach. Behind her, across the deserted earth stretches the trail of bare feet, the wake of suffering and death. The bones of the old people and the young children have been sown across this earth with, for their only sepulture, the crevices in the rocks, the ravines where vipers dwell. Over the brackish wells hang the remnants of her people, rags upon the thorns of the acacia trees. Those who could not, would not, walk any farther. Those who no longer believed in the dream. And each day, at the zenith, the priests' voices echo across the desert, telling the people of Meroë that their queen is once again on her way towards the setting sun.

One day, however, she called for her scribes and her seers. She dictated her last wishes. They wrote her vision on a scroll of dried paper for the last time: the city of peace, spread across the river like an immense raft. That which she has kept in her heart since losing her sight, that which can only appear clearly when the light of the setting sun touches her face, now unveils its resplendent route to her. She now knows she will never attain her dream. The river will remain unknown. Now she knows she will enter another world, cold and fleshless, where the sun does not rise. To her daughter Arsinoë she has given her vision. Still a child, she has become the new queen of the people of Meroë. On her forehead of black stone, in the secret of the sacred tent, the priests of Osiris have attached the divine sign, the powerful drawing of the winged disc. Then they excised her so that in her pain she would always be the bride of the sun.

The people of Meroë have begun to walk again, and now it is the young queen Arsinoë who goes before them on their way. Like a river of bone and flesh the people flow over the red earth, deep within the crevices, into the desiccated valleys. The immense, red sun rises to the east, and a haze of sand is above the earth.

Like a river, the people of Meroë flow past the shelter of branches and canvas where Amanirenas lies in the shade at the entrance to the kingdom of the dead. She does not hear the crowd pass by, she does not hear the women's weeping, or the cries of the children, or the calls of their beasts of burden. Only the old priest has remained with her, sharing her blindness, the one who has always been her companion. He has kept a bit of water and some dates, to ease the wait for their passage. Amanirenas no longer hears his prayers. She feels the last palpitation leave her body and spread across the desert. On an oblique stone at the entrance to the hut a scribe has written her name. The warriors have built a wall of stone around the tomb so that the jackals cannot enter. They have suspended magic strips of cloth from the thorns of the branches. The human river has slowly flowed on, westward, and silence has returned, while the sun passes its zenith and begins its descent to the horizon. Amanirenas listens to the slowing of her heart, watches the patch of light within her eyes grow dimmer, like a fire going out. Already the wind is covering her face with dust. The old priest closes her eyes, places in her hands the insignia of power, between her ankles the box of the book of the dead. Amanirenas is no more than a trace, a mound lost in the vast, empty expanse.

Aro Chuku

The news had come, insidiously. Maou had figured everything out, before any of it was made known. She had awoken one morning at dawn. Geoffroy was asleep next to her, the skin of his bare chest covered with tiny droplets of sweat. A pale, faint daylight came in through the open shutters, lighting the space inside the mosquito net. Geoffroy slept with his head thrown back, and Maou thought, "We are going to leave this place, we can no longer stay. . . ." It was obvious, a thought which brought pain, like a decaying tooth suddenly reminding one of its presence. She also thought, "I must leave, I must take Fintan away before it is too late." Why should it be too late? She did not know.

Maou got up and went to drink from the filter in the pantry. Outside, on the veranda, the air was cool, the sky the color of pearl. Birds already filled the garden, hopping across the tin roofs, flying from tree to tree, chattering. Maou looked out towards the river. On the slope, white columns of smoke indicated the shacks where the women were cooking yams. She listened with an almost painful attentiveness to the sounds of ordinary life—cocks crowing, dogs barking, axes pounding, the motors of fishing pirogues backfiring, the rumble of lorries moving along the track to Enugu. She waited to hear the distant shuddering of the generator as it brought the sawmill to life, on the other side of the river.

She listened to everything as if she knew that she would no longer hear these sounds. That she would leave to go very far away, to forget the things and the people she loved, this town so far from war and cruelty, these people to whom she felt closer than to anyone before.

When she first came to Onitsha, she was something of a strange bird. Children walked behind her in the dusty streets, taunting her, calling out to her in pidgin, laughing. The first time, she remembered, she had run out without her hat, wearing the low-cut blue dress of the parties on board the *Surabaya*. She was looking for Mollie, the cat, who had been missing for two days; Elijah said he had seen her in a street in town, not far from the wharf. She went up to people, trying out her pidgin: "You seen cat bilong me?" Word had spread through town: "He don los da nyam." The women laughed. They answered, "No ben see da nyam!" That had been her first word, "nyam." Then the cat came home, already pregnant. The word had stuck, and when Maou walked by, she heard the echo as if it were her own name: "Nyam!"

She had never cared for anyone as much as she cared for these people. They were so gentle, their eyes so luminous, their gestures so pure and elegant. When she walked through the different neighborhoods to reach the wharf, children came up to her, not shy, and caressed her arms; women took her by the hand, spoke to her, in the gentle language which hummed like music.

She was even rather frightened in the beginning—such brilliant gazes, these hands touching her, pressing against her body. She was not used to it. She remembered what Florizel, on the ship, had told her. At the Club, too, they told the most dreadful stories. People disappearing, children abducted. The "Long Juju," human sacrifices. Pieces of salted human flesh sold at the market, in the bush. Simpson thought it great fun to frighten her, saying, "Fifty miles from here, near Owerri, there used to be the oracle of Aro Chuku, the center of sorcery for all of the west, where they preached holy war against the British Empire! Piles of skulls, altars smeared with blood! Do you hear the drums at night? Do you know what they are saying, while you sleep?"

Gerald Simpson made fun of her, of her inquisitive outings to town, of her friendship towards the fishermen's wives, the market vendors. Then, after she had taken up the defense of the convicts digging his swimming pool, he looked upon her with disdain and hostility. She did not behave like the wife of a civil servant, in the shelter of garden parties, under a parasol, reigning over a ballet of servants. At the Club Geoffroy was subjected to Simpson's ironic gaze and his barbed remarks. Everyone knew that the position of United Africa's agent was more and more compromised as a result of the reports submitted by the D.O. "Everyone according to rank" was Simpson's motto. He viewed colonial society as a rigid structure in which all had to play their part. Naturally, he had reserved the most important role for himself, next to the Resident and the magistrate. The central pivot. "Weathercock!" corrected Geoffroy. Gerald Simpson could not forgive Maou for her independence and imagination. In fact, he feared the critical gaze she laid upon him. He had decided that Geoffroy and Maou would have to leave Onitsha.

At the Club, relations grew more and more tense. Perhaps they were waiting for Geoffroy to make a decision—repudiate the intruding woman, send her home to that Latin country whose accent, mannerisms, and even skin tone—too mat—she had, most outrageously, preserved. Rally, the Resident, had tried to warn Geoffroy. He was also aware of how intensely Simpson disliked Maou.

"Can you imagine how thick your file in London must be?"

He added, because he knew everything:

"You must realize . . . Simpson files a report every week. You should request your immediate transfer."

Geoffroy choked on the injustice. He came home, shattered: "There's nothing more I can do. In my opinion, they've commissioned Rally to read me my sentence."

It was the beginning of the rainy season. The big river was the color of lead beneath the clouds, the wind flattened the treetops with violence. Maou no longer left the house in the afternoon. She stayed on the veranda, listening to the rising storms, far off towards the source of the Omerun. Heat crackled the red earth before the rain. The air danced above the tin roofs. From where she sat she could see the river, the islands. She had lost all desire to write, or even to read. She needed only to look, to listen, as if time were of no more importance.

All at once she understood what she had learned in coming here, to Onitsha, and what she could never have learned elsewhere. Slowness, that was it, a very long and regular movement, like the water of the river flowing towards the sea, like the clouds, like the sweltering afternoon heat, when light filled the house and the tin roofs were like the walls of a furnace. Life came to a halt, as if time were weighted. Everything became imprecise, there was nothing left but the water flowing downstream, this liquid trunk with its multitude of ramifications, its sources, its streams secreted in the forest.

She remembered how, in the beginning, she had been so impatient. She thought she had never hated anything as much as this little colonial town—crushed by the sun, asleep on the shore of the muddy river. On the *Surabaya* she had imagined the savannah, gazelle-like people leaping through the wild grasses, forests resonant with the cries of monkeys and birds. She had imagined naked savages, painted for war. Adventurers, missionaries, doctors consumed by the tropics, heroic women school teachers. In Onitsha she had found a society of boring and sententious civil servants, dressed in ridiculous outfits and headgear, who spent their time playing bridge, drinking, and spying on each other, and their wives, cramped by their respectable principles, counting their pennies and speaking harshly to their maids, waiting for the return ticket to England. She thought she would hate these dusty streets forever, these poor neighborhoods with their shacks overflowing with children, this race of people with their impenetrable stare, and this caricature of a language, pidgin, which aroused in Gerald Simpson and the gentlemen of the Club such mirth, while the convicts dug the hole in the hill like a collective grave. No one escaped the harshness of her gaze, not even Dr. Charon or Rally, the Resident, and his wife, so kind and pale, with their little lap dogs, as spoilt as children.

Thus she lived in expectation of the hour of Geoffroy's return, walking nervously to and fro in the house, tending the garden, or going over Fintan's lessons with him. When Geoffroy came back from the offices of the United Africa, she would press him with feverish questions for which he had no answer. She would go to bed late, well after he did, beneath the white tent of the mosquito net. She would watch him sleep. She thought of the nights in San Remo, when they had their life before them. She remembered the taste of love, the shiver at dawn. All so far removed, now. The war had erased everything. Geoffroy had become another man, a stranger, the one Fintan spoke of when he said, "Why did you marry that man?" He had gone away. He no longer talked of his research, of the new Meroë. He kept it within, it was his secret.

Maou had tried to talk about it, to understand.

"She's the one, isn't she?"

"She?" Geoffroy looked at Maou.

"Yes, she's the one, the black queen, you used to talk to me about her. She's the one who has come into your life. There's no more room for me."

"Don't be silly."

"Yes, I assure you—perhaps I should go away with Fintan, leave you to your ideas, I disturb you, I disturb everyone here."

He had looked at her, confused; he no longer knew what to say. Perhaps she was mad, after all.

Maou stayed on, and slowly she entered the same dream, she became someone else. Everything she had experienced before Onitsha — Nice, Saint-Martin, the war, the waiting in Marseilles — all of it had become foreign and distant, as if someone else had experienced it.

Now she belonged to the river, to this town. She knew every street, every house, she knew how to recognize the trees and the birds, she could read the sky, guess the wind, hear every detail of the night. She knew the people too, she knew their names, their pidgin nicknames.

And then there was Marima, Elijah's wife. When Maou first arrived, Marima still seemed like a child, frail and timid in her brand-new dress. She stayed in the shadow of Elijah's hut, she dared not show herself. "She is frightened," explained Elijah. Bit by bit she had allowed herself to be tamed. Maou made her sit down next to her, on a tree trunk which served as a bench in front of Elijah's hut. She said nothing. She did not speak pidgin. Maou showed her magazines, newspapers. She liked to look at the photographs, the pictures of dresses, the advertisements. She held the magazine slightly to one side to see it better. She laughed.

Maou learned words in her language. *Ulo*, house. *Mmiri*, water. *Umu*, children. *Aja*, dog. *Odeluede*, it's soft. *Je nuo*, drink. *Ofee*, I like it. *So!* Speak! *Tekateka*, time is passing. . . . She wrote the words down in her poetry notebook, then read them out loud, and Marima burst out laughing.

Oya came too. At first, shyly, she would sit on a stone at the entrance to Ibusun, looking at the garden. Whenever Maou drew near, she ran away. There was something both wild and innocent about her at the same time which frightened Elijah, and he looked upon her as a witch. He wanted to chase her away by throwing stones at her, and he called her bad names.

One day Maou was able to approach her and take her by the hand; she led her into the garden. Oya did not want to go into the house. She sat outside on the ground, against the stairs leading to the terrace, in the shade of the guava trees. She stayed there with her legs crossed, her hands resting flat against her blue dress. Maou had tried to show her some magazines, as she had done with Marima, but Oya wasn't interested. She had a strange look in her eyes, smooth and hard as obsidian, full of an unfamiliar light. Her eyelids lifted up towards her temples, drawn with a fine edging exactly like the Egyptian masks, thought Maou. Maou had never seen a face of such purity — the arc of her eyebrows, the height of her forehead, her lips with the trace of a smile. And above all these almond-shaped eyes, the eyes of a dragonfly or a cicada. When Oya's gaze came to rest upon her, Maou shuddered, as if through her gaze were filtered thoughts extraordinarily distant and clear, images of a dream.

Maou tried to speak with her through sign language. She vaguely remembered certain gestures. Whenever, as a child in Fiesole, she passed the deaf-mute children from the hospice, she would look at them, fascinated. To say "woman" she pointed to her hair, to say "man," her chin. For "child" she made a gesture with her hand as if patting the head of a very small child. For other gestures she made things up. To say "river" she made the motion of flowing water, to say "forest" she spread her fingers in front of her face. In the beginning Oya looked at her with indifference. Then she too began to speak. It was a game that lasted for hours. On the steps of the staircase, in the afternoon, before the rain, it was a good time. Oya showed Maou all sorts of gestures to express joy, fear, to ask questions. Her face grew lively, her eyes shone. She made funny faces, imitated people, the way they walked, their comical expressions. She made fun of Elijah because he was old and his wife was so young. They both laughed. Oya had a particular way of laughing, soundlessly, her mouth opening over her very white teeth, her eyes narrowed like two slits. Or, if she was sad, her eyes would cloud over and she would curl into a ball, her head bent over, her hands on the back of her neck.

Now Maou understood almost everything, and she could talk to Oya. There were extraordinary moments, in the afternoon before the rain, when Maou felt she was penetrating another world. But Oya was afraid of people. When Fintan arrived, she would avert her head and would no longer speak. Elijah did not like her. He said she was bad, that she cast spells. When Maou learned that she lived at Sabine Rodes's house, that man she despised, she tried everything to make Oya leave his house. She spoke about it to the Mother Superior at the convent, an energetic Irishwoman. But Sabine Rodes was beyond morality and propriety. All that Maou achieved was to exacerbate the man's unrelenting animosity. Maou thought it would be better not to insist, not to see Oya anymore. It was painful, so strange, something she had never felt before. Oya came nearly every day. She arrived noiselessly and sat on the steps; she would caress Mollie, waiting, her smooth face held up to the light. She seemed like a child.

It was the impression of freedom which was so attractive to Maou. Oya knew no constraints and viewed the world as it was, with the smooth gaze of a bird or a very young child. It was that gaze which caused Maou's heart to beat faster, and which disturbed her.

At times when she grew tired of speaking with gestures, Oya would let her head fall against Maou's shoulder. Slowly her fingers would caress the skin on Maou's arm, taking pleasure in brushing the fine hairs the wrong way. Maou stiffened at first, as if someone might see and start talking, then she grew used to this caress. Towards late afternoon everything was silent at Ibusun; the light was so soft, so warm, before the rain. It was like a dream; Maou recalled long-ago events from childhood, the summer in Fiesole, the warm grass and the buzzing of insects, the very soft fingers of her friend Elena caressing her bare shoulders, the odor of her skin, her sweat. Oya's odor troubled her, as did, when she turned towards her, the brilliance of her eyes against the shadow of her face, like living jewels.

In this way, one day Oya made her feel the child she was carrying in her belly; she guided Maou's hand through the low opening in her dress to the place where the fetus rippled, almost imperceptibly, as light as a nerve trembling beneath the skin. Maou left her hand for a long time against Oya's full belly, not daring to move. Oya was soft and warm, and as she had leaned against her, it seemed she was sleeping. Then a moment later, for no reason, she jumped up and ran off down the dusty road.

Perhaps it was because of Oya that Maou learned to love the rain. Her hands opened before her face, as if she were the one to open the floodgates of the sky. *Ozoo*, the rain which came from upriver at the speed of the wind, covering the parched earth with a beneficent shadow.

At the end of each afternoon, after Oya's departure, Maou would watch the rain's arrival; it was dramatic. There were muffled bursts of thunder from the direction of the high plateau where the sky was black as ink. They no longer needed to count the seconds. Fintan sat next to her on the floor on the veranda. She looked at his burnt face, his tangled hair. He had her forehead and her thick hair, a "bowl" cut that made him look like an American Indian. He was no longer the withdrawn, fragile child who had stepped off the ship onto the quay at Port Harcourt. His face and his body had grown hard, his feet were wide and strong like those of the children from Onitsha. There was above all something changed in his physiognomy, in the way he looked at people, in his gestures, which proved that the greatest adventure in life, the passage to adulthood, had begun. It was terrifying; Maou did not want to think about it. Suddenly she drew Fintan to her, as hard as she could, as if it were a game. He tried to pull away, laughing. For a few moments he was still a child.

"Your legs are all scratched, look, where have you been running to?"

"Over there, towards Omerun."

"You always go with Josip? Bony, I mean."

He looked away. He knew Maou was afraid when he left with Bony.

"Don't go too far, it's dangerous — you know your father already has a great many worries."

"Him? He knows nothing about it."

"Don't say that — he loves you, you know."

"He's a nasty man, I hate him."

He pointed below his shoulder to a black and blue mark on his arm.

"Look, *he* did that, with his stick."

"You must obey him, he doesn't like you to be out at night."

126

Fintan persisted in his spite.

"But I broke his stick, he'll have to go cut another."

"And if a snake bites you?"

"I'm not afraid of snakes. Bony knows how to speak to them. He says he knows their chi. He knows the secrets."

"And what are they, these secrets?"

"I can't tell you."

The rain fell on the tin roof with a metallic clatter. At once there was a gust of cold air from deep within the river. The noise was so loud that they had to shout in order to speak. The earth was furrowed with red rivulets.

In the evening she would take out the manuals and exercise books to work with Fintan. There were maths, geography, English grammar, French. She sat in the rattan chair and Fintan sat on the floor, on the veranda. Even when the rain lessened it was difficult to work. Fintan looked at the curtain of rain and listened to the splattering of drops, the water cascading into the canvas-covered drums. When he had finished working, he would go to fetch a book that he particularly liked. It was a very old little book that he had found in Geoffroy's library; it was called The Child's Guide to Knowledge. It was entirely made up of questions and answers. Fintan handed it to Maou, so that she would translate excerpts for him. There were answers to all sorts of questions, such as: "What is a telescope?"

"It is an optical instrument composed of several lenses enabling us to view faraway objects."

"Who invented it?"

"Zacharie Jansen, a Dutchman from Middleburgh, in Zeeland, an eyeglass maker by trade."

"How did Jansen invent it?"

"Absolutely by chance. He happened to place two lenses at a certain distance from one another and realized that the two lenses, in such a position, enlarged objects considerably."

"How did he proceed?"

"He fixed the lenses in that fashion, and in 1590 he manufactured the first telescope of a length of twelve inches."

"And who improved upon his invention?"

"Galileo, an Italian born in Florence."

"Did he suffer from his studies and the constant usage of glasses?"

"Yes, because he went blind."

When she had finished with the Guide to Knowledge, Fintan asked, "Maou, speak to me in your language."

The light was dim, night was falling. Maou rocked to and fro in her rattan chair, singing filastrocche, ninnenanne, softly at first, then more loudly. It was strange to hear these songs and the gentle sound of the Italian language mingling with the sound of the water, the way it used to be in Saint-Martin.

She recalled that when they first arrived she had taken Fintan to a reception at the Residency. Tea and cake were served in the garden. Fintan ran up and down the paths, and the little dogs were barking. Maou had called to Fintan in Italian. Mrs. Rally came over and said, in her timid little voice, "Excuse me, but what sort of language are you speaking?" Later, Geoffroy reproached Maou. Lowering his voice to show that he was not shouting—perhaps also because he knew full well he was wrong—he said: "I do not want you to speak to Fintan in Italian, particularly at the Resident's house." Maou replied: "And yet you used to like it, once." Perhaps it was from that day on that everything changed.

There was the sound of the V8 in the night. It resounded, despite the clamor of the storm, as if it came from afar, an airplane escaping the tempest. Fintan crawled in under his mosquito net. If Geoffroy found him still up, there would be trouble yet again.

Maou waited on the veranda. There was the sound of footsteps in the garden, wooden steps creaking. Geoffroy was pale, he looked tired. Rain had soaked his shirt and plastered his hair, making the bald spot on the top of his head appear larger.

"It came this afternoon."

He held out a sheet of rain-splattered paper. It was a letter giving him notice: Geoffroy would no longer be employed by the United Africa Company. Just a few lines from the management to say that his contract was not being renewed. A decision with no justification and therefore without appeal. Maou felt a kind of relief, and at the same time she wanted to cry. Now, they would have to leave.

To restrain her emotion, she said: "What are we going to do?"

"Leave, I suppose." Then he grew angry: "I wired London! I won't be pushed around without having my say!"

He thought of his research, the road from Meroë, the foundation of the new empire on the island in the middle of the river. There would not be enough time.

Sitting on the veranda, he looked again at the letter in the lamplight, as if he had not finished reading it.

"I shan't leave. We have the right to stay on here for a bit."

"How long?" said Maou. "If nobody wants you to stay?"

"And who decides upon that?" exclaimed Geoffroy. "I'll go elsewhere, to the north, to Jos, Kano."

But he knew quite well that that would not be possible. He sat on in the armchair, watching the falling rain. There were no other lights. The river was invisible.

In his bed, Fintan was not asleep. He lay staring at a ray of light on the ceiling; it came in from the veranda through a slit in the shutter.

"Come," said Bony.

He knew that Fintan would leave some day, that they would not meet again. He hadn't said anything, but Fintan understood—from the way he looked at him, from his haste, perhaps. Together they ran across the great field of grass, down to the Omerun. The gray of dawn still clung to the trees, smoke rose from the houses. Birds flew up out of the tall grass, whirling into the sky with their piercing cries. Fintan liked to go down to the stream. The sky seemed immense.

Bony ran forward, in grass taller than he was. From time to time Fintan glimpsed his black form gliding ahead of him. They did not call to each other. There was only the sound of their breathing, resonant in the silence, a hissing sound, slightly hoarse. When Fintan lost Bony from sight, he looked for the trail, the flattened grass, sniffing for his friend's odor. He knew how to do this now: walk barefoot with no fear of ants or thorns, follow a trail by smell, hunt at night. He could sense the presence of animals hidden in the grass—guinea fowl hugging the trees, the rapid gliding of snakes, at times the acrid smell of a wild cat.

Today Bony was not headed for the Omerun. He was walking eastward, in the direction of the Nkwele hills, where the clouds began. Suddenly the sun appeared above the earth with a brilliant light. Bony paused for a moment. Squatting on a flat rock above the grass, his hands joined behind his neck, he looked ahead as if he were trying to remember the way to go. Fintan joined him and sat on the rock. The sun's heat was already burning, causing drops of sweat to break out on their skin.

"Where are we going?" asked Fintan.

Bony pointed to the hills, beyond the yam fields.

"Over there. We'll sleep over there tonight." He spoke in English, not pidgin.

"What is there, over there?"

Bony had a shining, impenetrable face. Fintan suddenly realized that he looked like Okawho.

"Over there is mbiam," was all he said.

Bony had already said this word a few times. It was a secret. He had said, "Some day you will come with me to the mbiam water." Fintan understood that that day had arrived because he would be leaving Onitsha. It made his heart beat faster. He thought of Maou, her tears, Geoffroy's anger. But it was a secret, there was no turning back.

They continued walking, one behind the other now. They crossed a chaos of rocks, then entered a thorny undergrowth. Fintan followed Bony and felt no fatigue. Brambles tore his clothes. His legs were bleeding.

Towards noon they reached the hills. There were a few isolated houses where dogs were barking. Bony climbed up a worn, dark gray boulder, which crumbled into shards under his feet. From the top of the rock they could see the entire expanse of the plateau, the distant villages, the fields, and, almost unreal, the bed of a river shining among the trees. But what drew their gaze was a great fault in the plateau where the red earth glowed like the edges of a wound.

Fintan looked at every detail of the landscape. There was a great silence here, only the light rustling of the wind on the shale, the thin echo of the dogs. Fintan dared not speak. He saw that Bony too was contemplating the expanse of the plateau, the red fault. It was a mysterious place, far from the world, a place where one could forget everything. "This is where he ought to come," thought Fintan, thinking of Geoffroy. At the same time he was astonished he no longer felt any rancor. This place obliterated everything, even the burning of the sun and the stinging of poisonous leaves; even thirst and hunger. Even beatings.

"The mbiam water is over there," said Bony.

They went down the slope of the hills to the north. The path was difficult, and the boys had to jump from rock to rock, avoiding thorny bushes and crevices. Before long they came to a narrow valley where a stream flowed. The trees formed a dark and humid vault. The air was full of mosquitoes. Fintan saw Bony's slim form ahead of him dodging through the trees. At one moment he felt his throat contract in fear. Bony had disappeared. He could hear only the beating of his heart. And so he began to run along the stream, among the trees, shouting, "Bony! Bony!"

At the base of the ravine the little stream flowed over the rocks. Fintan knelt at the water's edge and drank for a long time, his face against the water, like an animal. He heard a noise behind him and turned around with a shudder. It was Bony. He was walking slowly with strange gestures, as if there were a danger.

He led Fintan a bit higher up, along the stream. Suddenly, as they rounded a tree, there appeared the mbiam water. A deep pool, surrounded by tall trees and a wall of lianas. At the very extremity of the pool was a source, a small waterfall springing up among the foliage.

Fintan felt a pleasant coolness. Bony stopped by the pool and looked at the water, without moving. His face expressed a mysterious joy. Very slowly he lowered himself into the pool and washed his face and his body. He turned to Fintan: "Come!"

He took the water in his hand and sprinkled Fintan's face. The cold water ran over Fintan's skin, seeming to enter his body, to wash away his fatigue and his fear. There was a peace within him, like the weight of sleep.

The trees were immense and silent. The water was smooth and dark. The sky grew very light as always just before nightfall. Bony chose a spot, a small patch of sand on the shore, by the pool. With branches and leaves he made a shelter for the night, to protect them from the morning dew. There they slept, by the calmness of the water. In the early morning they returned to Onitsha.

Geoffroy keeps his eyes open in the night. He sees the light of his dream. It is in this light that the river appeared to the people of Meroë, far away in the middle of the savannah, a river like a dragon of metal. In winter the wind burns the red sky, the sun is at the center of its halo, like the queen among her people. Before dawn there is a sound, faint and sudden. The young men who go out each night as scouts have returned in haste. They tell how from a rock on which they climbed to chase partridges they discovered an immense river reflecting the light of the sky. And so the people of Meroë, who had set up camp to shelter from the sandstorm, begin to walk again. The men and the children leave first, abruptly; the priests carry the young queen's litter. All have left their belongings behind, their provisions, cooking utensils; the old women have stayed with the herds. There is a sound of footsteps in the crunching sand, a sound of breathing. All day they walk, without stopping.

They come to the edge of a cuesta and they stop, rigid with surprise. Soon the sound of voices grows louder, rising like a chant: the river! echo the voices of the people of Meroë, the river! Look, it's the river! They have reached the end of their journey, after such a long time, so many dead; they have arrived at Ateb where the river of the sky takes root.

Surrounded by priests, Arsinoë too looks at the river shining in the light of the setting sun. For a moment yet the disc is suspended above the horizon, enormous, blood red. As if time had ceased, as if nothing more would ever change, as if there would be no more death, ever.

At this moment, the people of Meroë have returned to the day of departure when Amanirenas, surrounded by the seers and high priests of Aton, announced the beginning of the journey to the other side of the world, to the gate of Tuat, to the land pierced by the sun. It is the same trembling, the same sound, the same chant. Arsinoë remembers. She was very small then, her mother was still young and full of strength. The route joining the two sides of the world is infinitely short, as if those two sides were only the front and back of a mirror. The rivers meet in the sky, the great god Hapy, color of emerald, flowing endlessly to the north, and this new god of mud and light splitting the yellow grass of the savannah and gliding slowly to the south.

At the place where they first saw the river, at the edge of the cuesta, the priests of Meroë raise a stele, to face the setting sun. With scissors they carve into the stone the name of Horus, master of the world, creator of the earth and the abysses. On the side of the setting sun, where the disc paused for so long, they carve the sign of Temu, the winged disc. In this way the sacred mark was born, the sign each newborn child must receive, in memory of the people of Meroë's arrival on the shores of the river.

The young queen Arsinoë is the first to receive the mark of Osiris and Horus. The last high priest already died long ago and was buried in the tomb of Amanirenas in the middle of the desert. It is a Nuba from Alwa, named Geberatu, who carves the sacred signs: on the forehead the two eyes of the bird of the sky, representing the sun and the moon, and on the cheeks the slanting stripes of the plumes of the falcon's wings and tail. He carves the face of the queen with the ritual knife and sprinkles the marks with copper filings. That very night all the firstborn children, boys and girls, receive the same sign, so that no one may forget the instant when the god paused in his walking and illuminated the bed of the great river for the people of Meroë.

But they have not reached the end of their journey. On rafts of reeds the people of Meroë have begun to descend the river in search of an island where they might found the new city. The strongest men and women leave first, surrounding the queen's raft. Along the shores the herds walk slowly, guided by children and old men. Geberatu takes with him a piece of the stele in order to found the future temples. On the sparkling river at dawn dozens of rafts glide slowly, restrained by the long poles dipped into the mud.

Every day the river seems wider, the shores more heavily laden with trees. Arsinoë sits beneath the canopy of leaves and looks at these new lands, seeking to uncover a sign of fate. Sometimes great, flat islands appear on the surface of the water, they too similar to rafts. "We must go further down," says Geberatu. At twilight the men of Meroë stop on the beach to implore the gods: Horus, Osiris, Thoth, who wears the eye of the celestial falcon, Ra, the master of the horizon to the east of the sky, the guardian of the gate of Tuat. Geberatu burns incense above the fires and reads the future in the curling smoke. Together with the Nuba musicians, who play the drum, he chants and swings his head, causing his cowrie necklaces to click together. His eyes roll backwards, his body forms an arc above the ground. Then he speaks to the god of the sky, to the clouds, the rain, the stars. When the fire has consumed the incense, Geberatu removes the soot and marks his forehead, his eyelids, his navel, and his toes. Arsinoë waits, but Geberatu does not yet see the end of the journey. The people of Meroë are exhausted. They are saying, "Let us stop here, we can walk no further." Every morning, at dawn, just as Amanirenas had done, Arsinoë gives the signal for departure, and the people of Meroë go again to the rafts. At the prow of the first raft, before the young queen's canopy, Geberatu is standing. His thin, black body is cloaked with a leopard-skin coat, and he carries the long harpoon spear as a sign of his magic. The people of Meroë murmur that the young queen is under his power now, that he even reigns over her body. Sitting in the shade of the leafy roof, her face turned towards the endless shore, she sighs, "When will we be there?" And Geberatu replies, "We are on the raft of Harpocrates, the sacred scarab is by your side, at the stern Maat, the father of the gods, is steering, wearing his ram's head. The twelve gods of the hours are propelling you to the place of eternal life. When your raft touches the island of the zenith, then shall we be there."

It is the river, flowing slowly down through Geoffroy's body while he sleeps. The people of Meroë pass through him, he feels their eyes looking to the shores obscured by trees. Ibises fly away before them. Every evening a bit farther; every evening the seer's incantation, his face frozen in ecstasy, the smoke of incense rising in the night. He seeks a sign among the stars, a sign in the thickness of the forest. He listens to the cries of birds, watches the serpents' trails through the mud of the shore.

One day at noon the island in the middle of the river appears, reed-covered, like a big raft. This is how the people of Meroë know they have arrived. It is here, the place for which they have waited so long, here in the bend in the river. The end of the long journey—because there is no more strength, no more hope, nothing but an immense tiredness. In the wilderness of the island the new city of Meroë is founded, with its houses, its temples. It is the birthplace of the daughter of Arsinoë and the priest Geberatu, the child who will be called Amanirenas, or Candace, like her ancestor who died in the desert. Geoffroy dreams of her now, of Candace, the fruit of the union between the last queen of Meroë and the seer Geberatu. He dreams of her face, her body, her magic, her gaze upon a world where everything is beginning.

Her face, smooth and pure as a mask of black stone; the elongated shape of her head; her profile of unreal beauty, her lips forming a smile, the arc of her eyebrows rising from the root of her nose and curving high like two wings; and, above all, her long, narrow eyes, like the body of the celestial falcon.

She is Amanirenas, the first queen of the river, heiress to the Empire of Egypt, born so that the island might become the metropolis of a new world, so that all the people of the forest and the desert may unite beneath the law of the sky. But already her name is no longer in that distant tongue, scorched and severed by the crossing of the desert. Her name is in the language of the river, she is called Oya, and she is the very body of the river, the wife of Shango. She is Yemoja, the force of the water, the daughter of Obatala Sibu and Odudua Osiris. The black peoples of Osimiri were allied with the people of Meroë. With them they brought cereal, fruit, fish, precious wood, wild honey, leopard skins, and elephant tusks. The people of Meroë offered their magic, their science. The secret of metals, the manufacture of pots, medicine, the knowledge of stars. They gave the secrets of the world of the dead. And the sacred sign of the sun and moon and the wings and tail of the falcon are carved onto the faces of the firstborn children.

He sees her, she troubles his sleep. Oya glides at the bow of the long pirogue, her pole balanced in her hands. Now he recognizes her: it is indeed her, in him, crazed and mute, wandering the length of the riverbanks in search of her dwelling place. It is she that men spy upon in the reeds, she at whom the children throw pebbles, because they say she carries away the souls from the depths of the river.

Geoffroy Allen awakes suddenly. His body is soaked in sweat. The name Oya burns in his mind like a sign. Noiselessly, he slides out from under the mosquito net and walks along the veranda. At the bottom of the invisible slope Oya's body shines in the night, indistinguishable from the body of the river.

Geoffroy had not been back to the Club. Through old Moises, who worked at the wharf, he learned that rumor had a name, that of his replacement, who was to arrive by the next ship from Southampton. His name was Shakxon, he had worked at Gillett's of Cornhill, at Samuel Montagu's as well. It was thanks to Sabine Rodes that Moises knew all these details. For a man who never set foot in Onitsha's English circle he was remarkably well informed.

Then Maou did a mad, desperate thing. One afternoon, while Geoffroy was in the offices of the United Africa, she took Fintan to the other end of town, above the quay, where Sabine Rodes's house stood like a small fort with its high picket fence and its gate. Maou stood at the gate, holding Fintan by the hand. The low door to the left of the gate opened and Okawho appeared, almost naked, his marked face shining in the light. He looked at Maou with no other expression than a boundless ennui.

"May I see Mr. Rodes?" asked Maou.

Okawho went away without replying, silent and supple like a cat.

He reappeared and led Maou into the big collection room with its shutters that were permanently closed. In the obscurity, the African masks, the furniture, the pearl-studded vases shone strangely. Then Maou saw Sabine Rodes in person, seated in a chaise longue by a whirring fan. He was wearing his long, pale blue Hausa robe, smoking a cigar.

Maou had seen him only once, shortly after her arrival in Onitsha. She was astonished by the color of his skin, a waxy yellow which stood out against the darkness of the big room, in sharp contrast to Okawho's almost blue black skin.

As Maou and Fintan came in, he got up and pulled two chairs over for them. "Sit down, please, Mrs. Allen." Maou was rather surprised by his falsely polite tone. She said,

"Fintan, go and wait for me in the garden."

"Okawho will show you the kittens which were born last night," said Rodes.

He had a soft voice, but she detected at once a cruelty in his eyes. She thought he must know perfectly well why she had come.

Outside, in the garden, the sun was dazzling. Fintan followed Okawho around the big house. In the rear courtyard, near the kitchen, Oya sat on the ground in the shade of a tree. She was dressed in her blue mission dress, the one she had worn when they went on board the *George Shotton*. She was staring at a box lined with rags in front of her in which a tortoise-shell cat was feeding her kittens. She did not look away when Fintan drew near her. Beneath her dress her belly and breasts were swollen. Fintan stood looking at her without speaking. Oya turned her head. Fintan saw her eyes, extraordinarily big, elongated towards her temples. Her copper-colored skin was dark, smooth, and shining. Her hair was still knotted tightly into the same red scarf, and around her neck she wore the same cowrie necklace. For a moment she looked at Fintan with that madness in her eyes which made one dizzy. Then she returned to her contemplation of the cat and kittens.

In the collection room Maou sat with a heavy heart. Sabine Rodes was treating her with the most unbearable mockery. He called her "signorina," speaking now in Italian, now in French, rolling his rs the way she did. His words were hateful. He is even worse than the

140

others, thought Maou. Now she was certain that he was the one who had plotted Geoffroy's dismissal from the United Africa Company. "My dear signorina, you must realize we see people like your husband pass through here every day, people who think they are going to change everything. I'm not implying that he is wrong, any more than you are, but one must be realistic, one must see things as they are and not as one would like them to be. We are colonizers, not the benefactors of mankind. Have you considered what would happen if the English you are so openly scornful of were to withdraw their cannons and their guns? Have you thought of the blood bath which would ensue, and have you thought that they would begin with you, dear signorina, you and your son, despite all your noble ideas, all your fine principles and friendly chats with the women at the marketplace?"

Maou made an effort, pretending not to have understood. "Is there no chance, no possibility remaining?" What she wanted to say was: "Do something, say something in his favor—this is where he wants to live, he does not want to leave this country!" Sabine Rodes shrugged his shoulders, puffed on his cigar. He felt bored all of a sudden. "Okawho, the tea?" This woman's feelings, her somber gaze, her Italian accent, the effort she made to conceal her anxiety—it all annoyed him, it was just too pathetic. He turned to something else now, spoke about Geoffroy's quest, his obsession with Egypt. "You know, I'm the one who first spoke to him about the Egyptian influence in West Africa— the resemblances with the Yoruba myths, with Benin. I told him about the standing stones I saw on the banks of the river Cross, over towards Aro Chuku. When he first got here, I had him read all the books— Amaury Talbot, Leo Frobenius, Nachtigal, Barth, and Hasan Ibn Mohamed al Wassan al Fasi, known as Leo Africanus. I'm the one who spoke to him of Aro Chuku, the last shrine to Osiris—that was my idea. He told you that, didn't he? He told you who the people of Aro Chuku are, he told you he wants to go there?" He seemed to be in thrall to a certain excitement, sitting up on his chaise longue, calling out, "Okawho! Wa!", his voice transformed, sonorous. "Go fetch Oya, straight away!"

The young woman came into the room, followed by Fintan. With her back to the light her silhouette seemed very large, and her belly, dilated by pregnancy, made her look like a giant. She stopped on the threshold. Sabine Rodes went up to her and brought her over to Maou.

"Look at her, Signorina Allen, she is the one who haunts your husband, she is the goddess of the river, the last queen of Meroë! Obviously, she's utterly unaware of that. She is mad and mute. She arrived here one day out of nowhere, wandering along the river from town to town, selling herself for a spot of food, for a cowrie necklace. She moved on board the *George Shotton*. Look at her, doesn't she look like a queen?"

Sabine Rodes got up, took the young woman by the hand and led her closer to Maou. From the shadow of the door Okawho watched them. Maou was angry.

"Leave her alone, she is not a queen, and she is not mad. She is a poor deaf and dumb girl everyone takes advantage of, you have no right to treat her like a slave!"

"She is Okawho's woman now, I gave her to him." Sabine Rodes went back to sit in his armchair. Oya withdrew slowly to the door. She slipped outside, passing Fintan who stood watching.

"But I could have given her to your husband!"

He added, perfidiously, his blue eyes scrutinizing Maou, "Who knows whose child she carries in her belly."

Maou's face burned with anger.

"How can you! You have no sense of . . . of honor!"

"Honor!" he repeated, rolling his rs the way Maou did, "Honorrr!"

He was no longer bored. He could make his usual speech. He got

142

up, and the sleeves of his robe slid down along his arms: "Honor, signorina! Have a look about you! The days are numbered for all of us, all of us! For good people and bad, for honorable people and for those like me! The empire is finished, signorina, it's crumbling on every side, turning to dust; the great ship of empire is sinking, honorably! You speak of charity, don't you, and your husband lives in his dream world, and meanwhile everything is crumbling around you! But I shan't leave. I shall stay here to see it all, that's my mission, my vocation, to watch the ship go under."

Maou took Fintan's hand. "You are mad." Those were her last words in Sabine Rodes's house. She walked quickly to the door. In the garden Oya had gone back to sitting by the cat in her box.

When Geoffroy learned what had happened, what Maou had done, he became violently angry. His voice echoed through the empty rooms, merging with the rumbling of the storm. Fintan hid in the cement room at the end of the house. He heard Geoffroy's voice, harsh and cruel:

"It is your fault, it's what you wanted as well, you did everything you could so that we should have to leave."

Maou's heart pounded; her voice was stifled with anger and indignation, she said it was not true, that it was cruel; she wept.

Fintan closed his eyes. There was the pattering of rain on the metal roof. The smell of fresh cement was stronger than anything. He thought, "Tomorrow I shall go to Omerun, to Bony's grandmother's. I'll never come back. I'll never go to England." Onto the cement wall he scraped with a stone POKO INGEZI.

The fire burns stronger and clearer now that nothing protects him any more, now that nothing can get in the way of his dream. Geoffroy is slowly going up the River Cross in an overloaded pirogue, fighting the strength of the current swollen by the rains as it sweeps mud and broken branches in its wake. Rain fell on the hills during the morning, and the tributaries of the Cross have overflowed, staining with blood the water of the river. Okawho is seated forward in the pirogue. He hardly moves; from time to time he takes a bit of water and drinks from his hand, or splatters his face. He agreed to come with Geoffroy, to guide him as far as Aro Chuku. He did not hesitate for a moment. He said nothing to Sabine Rodes. He came to the quay in the morning and climbed into the Ford V8 bound for Owerri. He took no belongings for the trip. He has only his everyday khaki shorts and torn shirt.

Now the pirogue is headed upriver, carrying the passengers to Nbidi, to Afikpo, to the lead mines of Aboinia Achara. Women and children, laden with baggage; men escorting goods, oil, petrol, rice, tins of corned beef, and concentrated milk. Geoffroy knows that he is going towards the truth, towards the heart. The pirogue goes up the river, towards the path of Aro Chuku, going back against the flow of time.

In the month of December 1901, Colonel Montanaro, commanding officer of the British forces in Aro, went up this same river on a steamboat carrying 87 English officers, 1550 black soldiers, and 2100 bearers. Then through the savannah, divided into four columns, the army began its march towards

144

Aro Chuku from Oguta, Akwete, Unwuna, Itu. A veritable expeditionary corps, as in Stanley's time, with surgeons, geographers, civilian officers, and even an Anglican priest. They are bearers of the power of the empire, they have orders to go forward, whatever the cost, to reduce the pocket of resistance that is Aro Chuku, to destroy forever the oracle of the *Long Juju*. Lieutenant Colonel Montanaro is a thin man, still pale despite years spent under the African sun. The orders are intransigent: destroy Aro Chuku, reduce to nothing the rebel city with its temples, its fetishes, its sacrificial altars. Nothing must remain of this cursed place. They must kill all the men, including the old men and the male children over ten years old. Nothing must remain of this rabble! Is he deliberating his war orders against the Aro people, against the oracle which preaches the destruction of the English? The four columns move forward through the savannah, guided by scouts from Calabar, Degema, Onitsha, and Lagos.

Is that what Geoffroy has come to search for, as if it were some sort of confirmation of the imminent end of the empire, or the end of his own African adventure? Geoffroy recalls his first journey back through time, when he first arrived in this country. The trip on horseback through the bushes of Obudu, to the dark hills where the gorillas live, in Sankwala, Umaji, Enggo, Olum, Wula; the discovery of the temples abandoned in the forest, the standing stones like giant phalluses against the sky, the steles carved with hieroglyphics. He wrote a long letter to Maou to tell her he had found the end of the route to Meroë, the signs left by Arsinoë's people. Then the war came, and the trail was lost to him. Will he be able to find it all again? As the pirogue heads upriver, Geoffroy inspects the shore, searching for a clue in which to recognize himself. Aro Chuku is the truth and the still beating heart. Light surrounds Geoffroy, spinning around the pirogue. Sweat causes Okawho's face to shine, and his scars seem open.

They have landed on the beach in the late afternoon, in a place where the River Cross forms an elbow. Okawho says that it is here that the path to Aro

Chuku begins. Somewhere on the opposite shore are the standing stones, hidden in the forest. Geoffroy lays out his belongings for the night, while the pirogue moves off again, carrying its cargo of men and merchandise upriver. Okawho sits on a stone and watches the water, saying nothing. His face is sculpted, a black and brilliant stone. His eyes are veiled by his heavy eyelids, his lips are arced in a half smile. On his forehead and his cheeks the *itsi* signs glow as if the copper powder had come alive with color. On his forehead, the sun and the moon, the eyes of the celestial bird. On his cheeks, the plumes of the wings and tail of the falcon. When night falls, Geoffroy wraps himself in a sheet to protect himself against mosquito bites. The beach echoes with the sounds of the river. He knows he is very near the heart, very near the reason for all journeying. He cannot sleep.

After the torrential rains and the tornadoes of July, there was a calm period in the month of August, known as the "little dry season."

Geoffroy had taken advantage of that time to go to the east. In the morning, when Fintan got up, he saw the clouds suspended above the river. The red earth was already cracking, forming clumps, but the river continued to ferry its load of silty water, dark and violet, clogged with trunks torn from the shores of the Benue.

Fintan had never imagined that this little season would bring him such happiness. Perhaps it was because of Omerun, the village, the river. In the afternoon Maou would rest in her room with the shutters closed, while Fintan ran barefoot through the savannah to the big tree where Bony waited for him. Before reaching the spot, Fintan could hear the soft music of the zanza, mingling with the chirring of insects. It was like a music to call the rain.

On the side of the giant fault, over by Agulu, Nanka, and the river Mamu, clouds gathered, forming a mountain range. There was smoke in the plain, above the villages and farms. Fintan could hear dogs yapping every now and again, calling each other from across the fields. While he walked on to the tree Fintan listened, looked around him with a sort of eagerness, as if it were for the last time.

Geoffroy had left, he had taken the road to Owerri. Perhaps he had gone to look for another house, since his replacement was going to take their place at Ibusun? But he had also spoken of that strange place, that mysterious, magical city in the middle of the savannah, Aro Chuku. Before climbing into the V8 he had behaved very strangely. He had hugged Fintan to him, very hard, running his hand through the boy's hair. At the same time he had said, very quickly, very softly, "I'm sorry, boy, I shouldn't have got angry. I was tired, do you under-stand?" Fintan felt his heart was beating too fast, he no longer knew what to think, it was as if he wanted to cry. Geoffroy whispered again: "Goodbye, boy, look after your mother, won't you?" Then he climbed into the car and folded his tall body behind the wheel. He had put a briefcase on the seat next to him, just as when he used to leave on business for Port Harcourt. "Is he going away for always?" asked Fin-tan. But already he regretted his question.

Maou had spoken of Owerri, Abakaliki, Ogoja, people he was going to see, the house they were going to find there. For the first time she said "your father." So perhaps they would be able to stay, perhaps they would not go back to Marseilles. The V8 went along to the road in a cloud of red dust, then down the slope, before being swallowed up by the streets of Onitsha.

The big tree was at the top of a rise overlooking the valley of the Omerun. Bony was sitting on the roots, playing the zanza, looking off into the distance. He had changed since his brother's imprisonment. He no longer went to Geoffroy's house, and when he ran into Fintan in town, he would go off in a different direction.

He knew Geoffroy had gone away. He said, Owerri, Aro Chuku. Fin-tan was not even surprised. Bony knew everything, as if he could hear people talking from a distance.

Fintan never talked to him about Geoffroy. Only once, after the night they spent outside, by the mbiam water, when Geoffroy had whipped Fintan with his belt. Fintan had shown Bony the marks on his legs and

148

back. He had said, "Poko ingezi," and Bony too found it great fun to say, "Poko ingezi."

Fintan liked Omerun. Bony's grandmother's hut was by the stream. The old woman gave them food, foufou, roasted yams, sweet potatoes cooked in ashes. She was a little woman, with an extraordinary name in view of her corpulence; she was called Ugo, the bird of prey which flies in the sky—a falcon, an eagle. She called Fintan "umu," as if he too were her son. Sometimes Fintan thought that this was truly his family, that his skin had become like Bony's, black and smooth.

Maou was still asleep under the tent of the mosquito net in the room with the half-opened shutters. Fintan slipped in, barefoot, to look at her, holding his breath for fear of waking her. It was in this way that he loved her the most, in sleep, with her brown curls tangled upon her cheeks and the reflection of the dawn upon her shoulders. It was like in the old days in Saint-Martin; it was like the time they were alone, the two of them, in the cabin of the *Surabaya*.

Since Geoffroy had left to go off towards Owerri, towards the River Cross, everything had changed. There was an extraordinary peace in the house, and Fintan no longer even wanted to go out. The world had come to a halt, had fallen asleep with the same sleep as Maou, and for that reason even the rain had ceased to fall. Everything was to be forgotten. There was no more Club, no more wharf, the warehouses of the United Africa were locked. Nor did Maou have any desire to go down to the town. It was enough to be up on the terrace and watch the river flowing, or to read Fintan's lessons to him, making him repeat his multiplication tables, his English irregular verbs. She had even begun again to write poetry in her notebook, about the river, the market, the fires, the smell of frying fish, of yams, of overripe fruit. She had so much to say that she did not know where to begin. But it was rather sad too, because she felt haste and impatience as she had in the days preceding her departure from Marseilles. And now where would they go when they left?

Bony no longer came to their meetings by the tree. It was because of the yam festival. In Omerun, Eze Enu reigns, he who lives in the sky and whose eye is Anyanu, the sun. He is also called Chuku abia ama, he who floats on the air like a white bird. When the clouds break apart, said Bony, miming at the same time with his arms a gliding bird, it is time to feed Eze Enu. We give him the first yam, all white, on a white cloth spread on the ground. On the cloth we place a white eagle's feather, a white guinea fowl's feather, and the yam, white like foam.

The festival was to begin that very evening. Marima asked Maou to go with her to Omerun to see the "game of the moon." It was a mystery. Neither she nor Maou had ever been there.

From his observation point on the old wooden pier Fintan watched the movement of boats along the river. Barges laden with drums of oil progressed slowly, drifting over tidepools, restrained by the men armed with their long, supple poles. From time to time a pirogue plowed through the water with a roar of outboard motor, its shaft projected far behind it like a frenetically waving arm. Farther upstream the islands seemed to be swimming against the current: Brokkedon, the wreck of the *George Shotton*, and, at the mouth of the Omerun, the large island of Jersey with its dark forest. Fintan thought about Oya, her body sprawled out in the wreck, her eyes seeking a spot behind her, while Okawho penetrated her; then the young warrior's anger, the sound of thunder while he broke the mirror. Fintan thought about the beach among the reeds, when Bony had tried to force himself upon Oya on the path—the anger he had felt, like a burning in his body, and the trace of Oya's teeth on his hand.

Because of everything that had happened, Fintan no longer believed they would leave Onitsha or return to Europe. It seemed to him that he was born here, by this river, under this sky; that he had always known this place. It was the slow power of the river, the water flowing, eternally, the water dark and red, carrying water like a body, Oya's body shining and swollen by pregnancy. Fintan watched the river, his heart beating, and he felt within him a part of the magical power, a part of the happiness. Never again would he be a stranger. What had happened there, on the wreck of the *George Shotton*, had sealed a pact, a secret. He remembered the first time he had seen the young girl, on the beach of Omerun, naked in the river. "Oya." Bony had uttered her name, very quietly. As if she were born of the river, color of the deep water, her smooth body, her breasts, her face with its Egyptian eyes. And they had remained lying on the bottom of the pirogue, mingling with the reeds, noiselessly, as if to surprise an animal. Fintan felt a tightness in his throat. Bony watched with a painful attentiveness, his face rigid like stone.

He would never be able to part with the river—so slow, so heavy. Fintan stood motionless on the pier until the sun went down on the opposite shore, the eye of Anyanu dividing the world.

The moon was high in the black sky. Maou was walking along the road to Omerun next to Marima. Fintan and Bony walked a few steps behind them. In the grass the toads made noise. The grass was black, but the leaves on the trees shone with a metallic brilliance, and the path glowed in the moonlight.

Maou stopped and took Fintan's hand.

"Look, how beautiful!"

At one point, at the top of the hill, she turned around to look towards the river. The estuary and the islands were clearly visible.

Other people were walking along the road to Omerun, hurrying to the festival. They came from Onitsha, or even the other shore, from Asaba, Anambara. Cycles wove their way past them, ringing their bells. From time to time a lorry punctured the night with its headlamps, stirring up a cloud of acrid dust. Maou had wrapped herself in a veil in the manner of the women from the north. The noise of footsteps swelled in the night. There was a glow from a fire somewhere in the village. Maou was frightened and wanted to say to Fintan, "Come, let's turn back." But Marima's hand pulled her along the road: "Wa! Keep walking!"

All at once she understood what had frightened her. The beating of drums had begun, somewhere to the south, mingled with the muffled grumble of an electric storm. But on this road, with these walking people, the noise was no longer frightening. It was a faint, familiar sound from the depths of the night, it was a human sound, reassuring like the lights from the villages shining along the river, to the edge of the forest. Maou thought of Oya, of the child who would be born here by the river. She no longer felt her solitude. It seemed that she had finally emerged from the confinement of colonial houses and their fences, where the whites hid away in order not to hear the world.

She walked quickly, with the hurried step of the people of the savannah. She had switched off her electric torch, the better to see the moonlight. She also thought about Geoffroy—how she would have liked him to be there with her, on this road, their hearts beating to the rhythm of the drums. It had been decided. When Geoffroy returned, they were going to leave Onitsha. They would take Oya and her baby away from Mr. Rodes, they would go away and say goodbye to no one. They would leave everything to Marima, everything they had, and they would go north. That was the saddest thing—that they would no longer see Marima's childlike face, no longer hear how she laughed whenever Maou recited her lessons in Ibo, *Je nuo, ofee, ulo, umu, aja,* and everything else she had learned with her while preparing the meals, outside on the stones of the hearth—*foufou,* cassava *gari, isusise,* boiled yams, and groundnut soup.

Maou squeezed Fintan's hand. She wanted to tell him right away: When Geoffroy comes back we'll go to live in a village, far away from all these nasty people, these indifferent, cruel people who wanted to ruin us and make us leave. "Where shall we go, Maou?" Maou wanted her voice to be jolly and carefree. She squeezed his hand harder. "We'll see, perhaps to Ogoja. Perhaps we'll go up the river as far as the desert. As far as possible." She dreamt as she walked. The moonlight was newly minted, sparkling, intoxicating.

When they arrived in the village, the square was filled with people. Cooking fires had been lit; there was a smell of hot oil and yam frit-

154

ters. There came the sound of voices, the cries of children running through the night, and, very close, the music of drums. Now and again the shrill notes of the zanza.

Marima led Maou through the crowd. Then suddenly they were at the heart of the festival. On the clearing of hard earth men were dancing, their bodies shining in the glow of the fires. They were young men, long-limbed and slim, wearing only ragged khaki shorts. They stamped the ground with the soles of their feet, their arms spread wide, their eyes bulging. Marima led Maou and Fintan away from the circle of dancers. Bony had disappeared into the crowd.

Standing against the wall of a house, Maou and Fintan watched the dancers. There were women dancing too; their faces spun into a blur, into dizziness. Marima took Maou's arm: "Don't be frightened!" she shouted. Maou had pulled her head in between her shoulders and pressed herself against the wall to hide in the shadow. At the same time she could not take her eyes off the silhouettes of the dancers among the fires. Then suddenly her attention was drawn to some men who were raising two posts on the square. Between the posts a long rope was stretched. One of the posts had the shape of a fork.

The drumbeats had not stopped. But the clamor of the crowd had gradually ceased, and the exhausted dancers lay down on the ground. Maou wanted to speak but her throat was constricted by a sort of incomprehensible anxiety. She held Fintan's hand very tightly. Against her back she felt the mud wall still warm from the sun. She saw that two figures were being hoisted onto each post, and at first she thought they were big rag dolls. Then the figures began to move, to dance seated upon the rope, and she realized that they were men. One was dressed in a woman's long robe and wore feathers on his head. The other was naked, his body streaked with yellow paint, dotted with white, and his face was masked by a large, wooden beak. Balancing on the rope, their long legs hanging into the void, they moved forward, writing to the rhythm of the drumbeats. The crowd had gathered beneath them, making strange cries, calling. The two men were like a pair of fantastic birds. They threw their heads back, spread their arms like wings. The male bird drew near with his beak, and the female bird turned, retreated in haste, then came back, to the laughter and shouting of the crowd.

There was something powerful drawing Maou to the spectacle of the bird-men. The music of the drums resounded now in the very core of her being, hollowing out a dizzy exhilaration. She was at the very heart of the mysterious drumming she had heard since her arrival in Onitsha.

The grotesque birds danced before her now, hanging from the rope in the light of the moon, bobbing their almond-eyed masks. Their movements were lascivious, then, all at once, they seemed to be fighting. Around her the spectators were also dancing. She saw the flash of light in their eyes, the hardness of their invulnerable bodies. In the middle of the square a curtain of flame undulated, and the men and children leapt through it, shouting.

Maou felt so frightened that she could scarcely breathe. She groped her way back to the wall of the house, searching for Fintan and Marima. The music of the drums pounded ever louder. The fabulous birds had united on the rope, forming a grotesque couple above their dangling, gigantic legs. Then they seemed to fall slowly and the crowd bore them away.

Maou trembled when a hand took her own. It was Marima. Fintan was with her. Maou felt like crying; she was so tired. "Come!" said Marima. She led her away, out of the village, onto the road which went up through the tall grass. "Are they dead?" asked Maou. Marima did not answer. Maou did not understand why it was all so important. It was merely a game in moonlight. She thought of Geoffroy. She felt the fever rise within.

Geoffroy is near the lake of life. Yesterday he saw the monoliths of Akawan-shi, on the shore of the Cross, erect in the grass like gods. With Okawho he went up to the basalt blocks. It was as if they had fallen straight from the sky to land erect in the red mud of the river. Okawho says they were brought from Cameroon by the power of the great magicians of Aro Chuku. One of the stones is as tall as an obelisk, thirty feet perhaps. On the side turned towards the west Geoffroy has recognized the sign of Anyanu, the eye of Anu, the sun, the hugely dilated pupil of Us-iri carried by the wings of the falcon. It is the sign of Meroë, the last sign written on the face of men in memory of Khunsu, the young god of Egypt who wore the drawings of the moon and sun tattooed on his forehead. Geoffroy remembers the words of the *Book of the Dead* as translated by Wallis Budge; he can recite them by heart, out loud, like a prayer, a shiver in the motionless air:

The city of Anu is like him, Osiris, a god.
Anu is like him, a god. Anu is as he is, Ra.
Anu is as he is, Ra. His mother is Anu.
His father is Anu, he himself is Anu, born in Anu.

The black stone is the most distant image of the god Min with his erect phallus. On the black side, the Ndri sign shines brightly in the low-angled light of the end of the day. Life whirls around the gods. There are insects hanging in the air, the red earth is etched with furrows. In a notebook Geoffroy

157

draws the sacred emblem of the queen of Meroë, *Ongwa* the moon, *Anyanu* the sun, *Odudu egbe*, the wings and tail of the falcon. Around the sign there are fifty-six dots carved into the stone, the halo of the Umundri, the children who surround the sun.

Okawho is standing next to the stone. On his face shines the same sign.

Then night falls. Okawho sets up a makeshift shelter against the rain.

The stars circle slowly around the black stones.

At dawn they continue to walk along the river. A fisherman's pirogue ferries them to the right bank of the Cross, a short way upstream from the monoliths. There they find a stream, half-blocked by the trees deposited by the last high water.

"Ite Brinyan," says Okawho. It is there, Atabli Inyang, the place where the lake of life is found. Geoffroy follows Okawho, who wades into the water, waist-high, beating a path through the branches with a machete. They move through the black, chilly water. Then they walk on rocks. The sun is high in the sky; Okawho has removed his clothes so that he will not be hindered by the branches. His black body shines like metal. He leaps forward, shows the way. Geoffroy follows with difficulty. His hoarse breathing resounds in the silence of the forest. The sun has been burning inside him, all these days, the sun burning at the core of his body, a supernatural vision.

What have I come here for? thinks Geoffroy, and can find no answer. Because of the tiredness, the burning of this sun deep within his body, all reason has blurred. All that matters is to go on, to follow Okawho into this labyrinth.

Shortly before dawn Geoffroy and Okawho arrive in Ite Brinyan. They have followed the narrow stream all day, hacking their way through the barrier of trees, crossing over the chaos of rocks along what was often no more than a corridor through the forest; suddenly it opens out, like a cave transformed into an immense subterranean hall. They stand before a lake which reflects the color of the sky.

Okawho has stopped on a rock. On his face there is an expression that Geoffroy has never seen on anyone's face. On a mask, perhaps—something hard and superhuman, the eyes emptied of all expression by thin circles drawn around them, the pupils dilated.

There is no sign of life either in the water or in the forest surrounding the lake. The silence is so great that Geoffroy thinks he can hear the sound of blood in his arteries.

Then, slowly, Okawho enters the dark water. On the other side of the bay the trees form an impenetrable wall. Some of the trees are so high that the sunlight still catches on their tops.

Now Geoffroy hears the sound of water. A sigh through the trees, through the stones. Following Okawho, Geoffroy goes into the lake and walks slowly towards the source. In the middle of the blocks of black sandstone is a waterfall.

"It is Ite Brinyan, the lake of life." That is what Okawho said, in a hushed voice. Or perhaps Geoffroy thought he heard him say it. He shivers before the water springing forth as in the first moment of the universe. It is cold. There is a slight breeze, a breath which comes from the forest.

In the bowl of his hands Okawho takes water and washes his face. Geoffroy crosses the lake, slipping on the rocks. The weight of his sodden clothes prevents him from climbing ashore. Okawho reaches out a hand and helps Geoffroy to pull himself onto the rocks surrounding the source. There Geoffroy washes his face and drinks at length. The cold water quells the burning at the core of his body. He thinks of baptismal ceremonies; he will never again be the same man.

Night falls. The silence is very deep, disturbed only by the voice of the source. Geoffroy lies down on the stones, which are still warm from sunlight. After so many trials, so much tiredness, it seems as if at last he has reached the goal of his journey. Before sleeping he thinks of Maou and Fintan. This is where he must come with them, to flee Onitsha, to escape betrayal. It is here that he will be able to write his book and finish his research. Like the queen of Meroë he has at last found the place of a new life.

At daybreak Geoffroy notices the tree. He had not recognized it—because of the darkness, perhaps. He was in its shadow and did not know. It is an immense tree, its trunk split in two, and its branches shade the water above the source. Okawho slept somewhat higher up, among its roots. On the ground near the trunk there is a primitive altar: broken jars, calabashes, a black stone.

All morning Geoffroy explores the area surrounding the source, looking for other clues. But there is nothing. Okawho is impatient, eager to leave again that very afternoon. They go back down the stream to the River Cross. On the shore, while waiting for the pirogue, they build a shelter.

During the night Geoffroy is woken by a burning all over his body. In the beam of the electric torch he sees that the ground is covered with fleas, so numerous that the earth seems to walk. Okawho and Geoffroy take refuge on the beach. In the early morning Geoffroy is shivering with fever and can no longer walk. He urinates a black liquid, the color of blood. Okawho wipes his hand over his face and says: "It's the *mbiam*. The water is *mbiam*."

At midday a pirogue with a motor stops off. Okawho carries Geoffroy on his back, then settles him under a canvas sheet to protect him from the sun. The pirogue moves quickly downstream towards Itu. The sky is immense, its blueness close to black. Geoffroy feels the fire flare up again in the core of his body, and the cold of the water rising in waves, filling him. He thinks, It is all over. There is no paradise.

When she felt that the moment had come, Oya left the community clinic and walked down to the river. It was dawn, and no one was about on the riverbanks. Oya was unsettled, searching for a place, as the tortoise-shell cat had done in Sabine Rodes's garden to have her kittens. At the quay she found a pirogue. She untied it and, pressing against the long pole, she pushed herself out into the middle of the river in the direction of Brokkedon. She was driven by haste. Already waves of pain were dilating her uterus. Now that she was on the water there was no more fear and the pain became more bearable. But in the clinic she had been locked up in the white room with all those sick women and the smell of ether. The river was calm, the morning mist clung to the trees, there were white birds in flight. Ahead of her the wreck was indistinct in the mist, fused with the island by the reeds and the trees.

She pushed the pirogue across the current, leaning with all her strength on the pole to gather momentum, and the pirogue continued on its own course, with a slight leeway. Oya was seized by a violent contraction. She had to sit down, her hands grasping the pole. The current bore her downstream, and she had to use the pole like an oar. The pain kept time with the movement of her arms, as they pressed the oars against the water. She managed to cross the current. She let herself go somewhat, moaning, hunched forward, while the pirogue slid slowly along the reeds, of Brokkedon. Now she was in the patch of calm water, bumping into the reeds from which clouds of mosquitoes arose. The prow of the pirogue touched the wreck at last. Oya ran her pole into the mud to immobilize the pirogue, then began to climb the old iron stairway to the deck. The pain obliged her to stop and catch her breath, her hands clutching the rusty railing. She sucked in the air, deeply, her eyes closed. When she left the clinic, her blue mission dress had stayed behind in the wardrobe; she had gone out in the white hospital gown now soaked in sweat and splashed with mud. But she had kept her tin crucifix. In the morning before dawn her waters had broken, and Oya had wrapped a sheet around her hips.

Slowly, on all fours, she crawled along the deck to the stairway which led to the ruined salons. There, by the bathroom, was her place. Oya undid the sheet and spread it on the floor, then lay down. Her hands felt for the pipes which ran along the walls. A pale light filtered through the openings in the hull, through the branches of the trees. The water of the river flowed along past the wreck, making a continuous vibration which entered her body and merged with the surge of her pain. Her eyes open to the light, Oya waited for the moment to come, while each wave of pain caused her to lift her body and close her hands around the old, rusted pipe above her. She sang a song she could not hear, a long vibration, like the movement of the river flowing past the hull, downstream.

Fintan and Bony went inside the wreck. They did not hear a sound except the rasping of her breathing, hoarse and oppressed. Oya lay with her back arched on the floor, in the old bathroom, her hands clinging to something which Fintan took at first for a branch, but which was the pipe from which Okawho had broken off a piece in order to smash the mirror. Bony also drew closer. There was a mystery here; they could only look and say nothing. When Fintan had arrived at the quay at dawn, Bony had told him everything—Oya's flight, the child about to be born. Bony had taken Fintan to the wreck in his uncle's pirogue. Bony did not want to climb up the iron stairway, but he followed Fintan. There was something terrible and compelling about it at the same time, and they stayed for a moment in the shadow, inside the hull, to watch.

At times Oya raised her body as if she were struggling, standing with her legs spread. She moaned softly in a high voice, like a song. Fintan remembered the time Okawho had held her down against the ground—the strange look in her eyes, her head thrown back as if she were in pain, and at the same time it was as if she were elsewhere. He tried to read her eyes, but the wave of pain was passing over her and she turned her head to one side, to the darkness. The white blouse from the clinic was splattered with mud and sweat, and her face shone in the half-light.

The moment had come now, after all those months of walking

through the streets of Onitsha with her unsteady step. Fintan sought Bony's eyes, but Bony had disappeared. Without a sound he had slipped outside, he had taken the pirogue and rowed ashore to look for the women from the clinic. Fintan was alone in the belly of the wreck, alone with Oya who was giving birth.

The moment had come. Suddenly she turned towards him, she looked at him, and he walked over to her. She held his hand so tightly, as if she would crush it. He too must do something, must take part in the birth. He did not feel the pain in his hand. He listened, he observed this extraordinary event. In the hull of the *George Shotton* something was imminent, filling the space, growing larger—a breath, water over-flowing, a light. Fintan's heart throbbed and ached, while the wave rolled over Oya's body, thrusting her face back, opening her mouth as if she were coming up for air. Suddenly she cried out, and the baby was thrust out onto the floor, a red glow in the nimbus of the placenta. Oya leaned forward and picked up the baby, and with her teeth she cut the cord. Then she lay back, her eyes closed. The child still shone with the waters of its birth; it began to cry. Oya pulled it towards her swollen breasts. Her body and her face shone too, as if she had swum in those same waters.

Fintan left the interior of the hull, walking unsteadily. His clothes were soaked in sweat. Outside, the river was like molten metal. The shores were blanketed by a white veil. Fintan saw that the sun was now at its zenith, and he felt a giddiness. So much time had gone by, some-thing so important, so extraordinary had taken place, and it had all seemed to him like a brief moment, a shiver, a cry. In his ears he still heard the ragged cry of the child; then Oya had guided the tiny body towards her breast, where the milk would flow. He could still hear Oya's voice, the song she alone heard, a moaning, the faint vibration of the river flowing around the hull. Fintan sat at the top of the iron stair-way and waited for Bony to return from the clinic with the pirogue.

164

The brief dry season was over. Once again there were clouds above the river. It was hot and close and the wind only rose towards the end of the day, after long hours of waiting. Maou no longer left the room where Geoffroy lay. She listened to the tin roof cracking in the heat of the sun and followed the rising of the fever in Geoffroy's body. He dozed, his waxen face overrun by beard, his hair sticky with sweat. She noticed that he was balding at the top of his head, and this was somehow reassuring to her. She imagined he must look like his father. At about three in the afternoon he opened his eyes, his expression emptied by fear. It was like a nightmare. He said, "I'm cold. I'm so cold." She gave him a glass of water to drink, with the tablet of quinine. It was the same struggle each time.

The first days after Geoffroy's return from Aro Chuku, Dr. Charon repeated the awful words, "Blackwater fever." Maou placed the bitter pill in Geoffroy's hand. She thought he was swallowing it with the water. But Geoffroy was getting worse. He could no longer stand. He was delirious. He thought that Sabine Rodes was coming into his room. He shouted incomprehensible words, curses, in English. He urinated with difficulty, black piss, pestilential. Elijah came to see him, looked at Geoffroy for a long time, then said, shaking his head, as if he were announcing a decision he regretted, "He's going to die."

Maou understood that Geoffroy was not taking the quinine tablets. In his delirium, he thought that Dr. Charon was trying to poison him. Maou found the tablets hidden under his pillow. Geoffroy was no longer eating. Drinking gave him stomach cramps.

The doctor came back with a syringe. After the first two injections of quinine Geoffroy was better. He agreed to take the tablets. The fits were less frequent, less terrifying. The hemorrhaging had ceased.

Fintan stayed in the house to be with Maou. He asked no questions, but in his eyes was the same apprehension. Maou said, "104 this morning." Fintan did not know the degrees in Fahrenheit, so she translated, "40."

On the veranda Fintan read the *Guide to Knowledge*. It was a fine thing. It was far removed from everything.

"What is the history of the printing press?"

"It is said that Laurentius Coster, from Haarlem, enjoyed sculpting letters in birch bark, and that is how he got the idea to print on paper with the help of ink."

"What is mercury, or quicksilver?"

"An imperfect metal, resembling liquid silver, very useful in industry and medicine. It is the heaviest liquid."

"Where is it found?"

"In Germany, Hungary, Italy, Spain, and South America."

"Is there not a famous mercury mine in Peru?"

"Yes, at Guanca Velica. It has been exploited for three hundred years. It is a veritable underground city, with streets, squares, and a church. Thousands of torches keep it lit, day and night."

Fintan liked to dream of all these extraordinary things — kings, marvels, fabulous peoples.

It was in the morning, before the rain, that the uprising broke out. Fintan understood right away. Marima came to warn them; there was a sort of fever all over town. Fintan went out of the house and ran along the dusty road. Other people were hurrying towards the town—women, children.

The uprising began at Gerald Simpson's house, among the convicts who were digging the hole for the swimming pool. The D.O. thought that everything would go back to normal and parcelled out a few wacks with his stick. The convicts seized one of the guards and drowned him in the hole full of muddy water; then, no one knows exactly how, some of them got free of their chain and, instead of running away, entrenched themselves at the top of the property, against the wire fence, and they were shouting and threatening the D.O. and the English guests at the Club.

Simpson realized that the situation was getting out of hand and took refuge inside the house with his guests. He rang up the Resident just before the mutineers pulled the post to the ground. The Resident sounded the alarm at the barracks.

Fintan arrived at the same time as the army vehicle. When he saw Simpson's house, a feeling of fear gripped his throat. The sky was so lovely, with its tufts of clouds, the trees so green—it seemed incredible that there could be such violence.

Lieutenant Fry arrived on horseback, and the soldiers took up their positions around the property in front of the great hole of muddy water. There was the sound of the convicts' voices, women's cries. Through a megaphone the lieutenant gave orders in pidgin made unintelligible by the echo.

On the terrace of the white house, the English guests surveyed the scene, half hidden by the colonnade. Fintan recognized Gerald Simpson's white jacket, his blond hair. He could see the Anglican priest, too, and people he did not know. Next to Simpson there was a podgy little man with a very white face crowned by a Cawnpore. Fintan thought it must be the man they had been waiting for, Geoffroy's replacement at the United Africa, with that odd name, Shakxon. All of them stood there, motionless, waiting for something to happen.

Inside the hole, by now, the convicts were no longer shouting or threatening. Those who had remained chained together stood in a group at the edge of the muddy water, their faces, glistening with sweat, turned towards the half circle of soldiers. The chain restraining their ankles gave them an aspect of robots halted in midmovement. Higher up, the convicts who had got free had drawn back as far as the fence. They tried to rip it out, in vain. There were a few places where the fence sagged like a belly. The convicts continued to shout out from time to time, but it was more like a death chant, a lugubrious, re-signed appeal. The soldiers did not move. Fintan's heart was thudding in his chest.

Then there were shouts. The spectators left the terrace and rushed into the house, knocking over the rattan chairs and tables. Fintan saw smoke coming from the direction of the muddy hole. The chained convicts were falling one on top of the other onto the ground. Fintan realized that what he had heard was gunshots. Bodies had fallen at the foot of the wire fence. One very tall black man, bare-chested, one of those who had led the mutiny, remained half hanging from the fence like a broken rag doll. It was terrifying — the smoke from the guns and now the silence, the empty sky, the white house abandoned by the spectators. The soldiers were running up the hill, their guns pointed ahead of them, and in an instant they were upon the convicts and had overcome them.

Fintan ran along the road, his bare feet striking the red earth, the air burning his throat as if he had screamed. At the end of the street he stopped, out of breath. His head was full of the sound of shooting.

"Come quickly!"

It was Marima. She took him by the arm and pulled him along. Her smooth face wore an expression which subjugated Fintan. There is danger, it said, we must not stay here. She took Fintan back to Ibusun. On the road, each time they met a group of men headed for the river, she would hide Fintan under a fold of her veil.

Maou was waiting in the garden, out in the sun. She was pale.

"I was so frightened, it's awful—what happened down there?"

Fintan tried to speak, he was sobbing. "They were shooting, they killed them, they shot the men in chains, they fell down." He clenched his teeth to keep from crying. He hated Gerald Simpson, the Resident and his wife, the lieutenant, the soldiers, and he hated Shakxon most of all. "I want to leave this place, I don't want to stay any more." Maou hugged him to her, caressing his hair.

Later that evening, after dinner, Fintan went to see Geoffroy. Geoffroy was in bed, in his pajamas, pale and thin. He was reading a newspaper in the light of the oil lamp, holding it right up against his face because he did not have his eyeglasses. Fintan saw the mark that the eyeglasses had left at the bridge of his nose. For the first time he thought that this was his father. Not a stranger, a usurper, but his own father. He had not met Maou by placing a notice in the newspaper, he had not drawn them into a trap by promising them riches. He was the one Maou had chosen, she loved him, she had married him, they had taken a honeymoon, in Italy, in San Remo. Maou had told him the story so often, in Marseilles; she had told him about the sea, the open carriages that drove along the seaside, the water so warm when they went bathing at night, the music in the bandstands. That was before the war.

"How are you, boy?" said Geoffroy. Without his glasses his eyes were a bright blue, very young.

"Are we going to leave soon?" asked Fintan.

Geoffroy thought for a moment.

"Yes, you're right, boy. I think it would be good to leave here now."

"And your research? And the story about the queen from Meroë?"

Geoffroy began to laugh. His eyes shone.

"Ah yes, you know about that? That's right, I did talk to you about all that. I ought to go north, to Egypt as well, and the Sudan. And then there are documents in the British Museum, in London. Then . . ." He hesitated, as if it were difficult to make sense of it all again. "Then we shall come back, in two or three years, when you'll be a bit farther along with your studies. We shall look for the new Meroë, farther upstream, in the place where the river makes a big W. We'll go to Gao, where it all began — Benin, the Yoruba, the Ibo; we'll look for manuscripts, inscriptions, monuments."

Suddenly the tiredness emptied his eyes and his head lay back against the pillow.

"Later, boy, later."

That night, before sleeping, Fintan snuggled his face into the hollow in Maou's neck, the way he used to, in the old days, in Saint-Martin. She caressed his hair, she sang nursery rhymes to him in Ligurian dialect, and the one he liked so much, about the Stura bridge:

> Al tram ch'a va Caïroli
> Al Bourg-Neuf as ferma pas!
> S'ferma mai sul pount d'la Stura
> S'ferma mai sul pount d'la Stura
> per la serva del Cura.
> Chiribi tantou countent quant a lou sent
> che lou cimenta!
> Ferramiu, ferramiu, ferramiu,
> Santa Giu!

At daybreak Okawho launches the long pirogue into the river. Oya sits at the prow, her favorite place. On her back, wrapped in a large, blue cloth, is her baby. From time to time she turns it round to her breast so that it can suckle. It's a boy; she doesn't know his name. He is called Okeke, because he was born on the third day of the week. The pirogue drifts slowly downstream, passing the piers where the fishermen wait. Okawho does not even turn around to look at Sabine Rodes's house, already in the distance, lost among the trees. When he came back from Aro Chuku, he bought the pirogue from a river fisherman; he got together a few provisions from the wharf—rice, dried fish, prawns, tins, an oil lamp, a few cooking utensils, and a length of cloth. Then he went to fetch Oya at the clinic and took her away with her son.

The pirogue glides in the current, effortlessly; Okawho hardly needs to use his paddle. The small craft is headed downriver, towards the delta, towards Degema, Brass, Bonny Island. To the place where the wave of the tide thrusts into the river, where swordfish and dolphins circle in the murky waters. The sun sparkles on the dark river. Birds fly up before the prow of the pirogue, fleeing towards the islands. Behind Okawho and Oya is the big town of planks and corrugated iron, the wharf, the sawmill, whose generator is beginning to hum. There are two large islands stretched along the surface of the water, and the carcass of the *George Shotton*, like some antediluvian monster. Already everything is vanishing into the distance, melting into the line of trees. When Okawho came back from Aro Chuku, he did not go to Sabine Rodes's house. He slept outside, near the clinic. He had already left, he was already far away, with Oya, in another world. Sabine Rodes did not understand. He walked through the town—he who never left his house except to go on the river—and he looked for Okawho by the wharf. He even dared to go to Ibusun, to spy. He questioned the sisters at the clinic. It was the first time that something, someone, was escaping him. Then, when he had finally understood, he locked himself into the big, gloomy room with its masks and its shutters forever closed, and he sat down in an armchair for a smoke.

The pirogue glides slowly through the water of the river. Okawho says nothing, he is used to silence. Oya has placed her son in the peak of the pirogue under a roof of branches, over which she has stretched the blue cloth. The sun climbs slowly into the sky, crossing the river as if on an immense, invisible ark. Day after day they navigate towards the estuary. The river is as vast as the sea. There is no more shore, no more land, only the rafts of islands lost in the swirling of the water. There on Bonny Island the huge petroleum companies—Gulf, British Petroleum—have sent their geologists to explore the river mud. Sabine Rodes saw them arrive one day on the quay—strange, bright red giants dressed in colored shirts and caps. No one had ever seen anyone like them on the river. He said to Okawho—but he might have been speaking to himself—, "The end of the empire." The foreigners set up camp to the south, at Nun River, Ughelli, Ignita, Apara, Afam. Everything is going to change. Pipelines will run through the mangrove; there will be a new town on Bonny Island; the world's largest cargo ships will come here; there will be towering chimneys, warehouses, giant reservoirs.

The pirogue slides through water the color of rusted metal. Clouds have risen above the sea, forming a tenebrous vault. Oya is standing, waiting for the rain. The curtain moves onto the river, erasing the shores. There are no more trees, no more islands—only water and sky merging into the moving cloud. Oya undresses and stands at the prow, her son pressed against her hip; her left hand holds the long pole against the stem of the pirogue. Okawho rows with his paddle, and they enter the curtain of rain. Then the storm is gone, upriver to the forest, to the grassy plains, to the faraway hills. When night falls, there is a red light on the horizon, by the sea, guiding the voyagers like a constellation.

On 28 November 1902 Aro Chuku fell to the English, almost without resistance. At daybreak the troops of Lieutenant Colonel Montanaro have met up in the savannah with the three other expeditionary corps, a short distance from the oracle. In the cool air of morning, with a very blue sky, their meeting looks more like a walk in the country. The black soldiers—Ibos, Ibibios, Yorubas—who had initially dreaded this expedition against the oracle of the *Long Juju,* feel reassured to see that the expanse of the savannah is empty. Drought has cracked the earth, and the yellowed grass is so dry that a spark could turn the prairie into an inferno.

Led by the scouts from Owerri, Montanaro's troops walk silently northward and bivouac on the banks of a stream, an affluent of the Cross. The oracle is so close now that in the evening the soldiers see the smoke of the houses and hear the muffled drumbeat of Ekwe, the great drum of war. In the night, strange stories begin to circulate in the mercenaries' camp. It is said that the *ofa* oracle has spoken, announcing the victory of the Aros and the defeat and death of all the English. When informed of these rumors, Montanaro, fearful of desertion, decides to attack Aro Chuku five days later, on 2 December. Once the oracle is surrounded, the cannons, which were dragged across the savannah, go into action. At dawn on 3 December, although not a single enemy has yet been seen, the first of Montanaro's troops attack the village, armed with Maxim machine guns and large-caliber rifles. A few shots are returned, and some mercenaries are killed. The Aros, their ammunition depleted, try to make a sortie, armed with only spears and swords, and are annihilated by the bursts of fire from the Maxims.

At about two o'clock in the afternoon, under a blazing sun, the troops of Lieutenant Colonel Montanaro enter the walls of the palace of Oji, the king of Aro Chuku. In the ruins of the dried-mud palace, eviscerated by shells, the leopard-skin throne stands empty. Next to it waits a child of ten, no older, who says his name is Kanu Oji, son of the king, and that his father lies dead beneath the rubble. The child, immobile and impassive despite the fear which widens his eyes, watches the troops go into what remains of the palace, pillaging ritual objects and jewels. Without a tear, without a word of protest, he goes to join the crowd of prisoners gathered before the ruins of the palace—women, old men, slaves, all thin and famished.

"Where is the oracle? *Long Juju?*" asks Montanaro.

Kanu Oji leads the English officers along a stream to a sort of creek surrounded by tall trees. There, in a ravine called Ebritum, they find the oracle that set all of West Africa ablaze: a large oval abyss, roughly seventy feet deep, sixty yards long, and fifty yards wide.

At the edge of a waterfall Montanaro and the other officers hack their way with their swords through two barriers of thorns. The water divides in a clearing, creating a rocky islet. On the islet stand two altars, one surrounded by rifles planted into the earth, the bayonets crowned with human skulls. The other altar, in the shape of a pyramid, bears the last offerings: jars of palm wine, cassava breads. On top of the rock is a reed hut, its roof covered with skulls. A deathlike silence hangs over the oracle.

Montanaro orders the altars to be destroyed with picks. Under the pile of stones they find nothing. The army torches the village houses and finishes levelling Oji's palace. The child watches as his father's house burns. His smooth face expresses neither hatred nor sorrow. On his forehead and cheeks shines the mark of the *itsi,* the sun and the moon and the plumes of the wings and tail of the falcon.

The last Aro warriors, prisoners of war, are led away to Calabar. Montanaro orders a great pit to be dug, and the bodies of the slain enemy warriors are thrown there along with the skulls which decorated the altars. The rest of the people—women, children, old men—form a long column, which sets off for Bende. From there the last Aros are scattered in the villages of the southeast—Owerri, Aboh, Osomari, Awka. Aro Chuku, the oracle, has ceased to exist. All that remains alive—on the faces of firstborn children—is the sign of the *itsi*.

They are not taken away to be slaves, they do not wear chains, for that is the privilege of the Umundri, the sons of Ndri. In memory of the pact, the first sacrifice, when on the bodies of the children the first nourishing crops had grown.

The English know nothing of that alliance. The children of Ndri begin their wandering, begging for food on the marketplace from town to town, travelling on the long fishing pirogues. Okawho grew up in this way, until he met Oya, who carries locked within the last message of the oracle, in anticipation of the day when it will be possible for everything to be born again.

On the trestle bed, Geoffroy listens to Maou's breathing. He closes his eyes. He knows he will not see that day. The road to Meroë has been lost in the desert sands. Everything has been erased, except for the sign of the *itsi* on the stones and on the faces of the last descendants of Amanirenas and her people. But he is no longer impatient. Like the flowing river, time has no end. Geoffroy leans towards Maou, and very close to her ear he murmurs, as in the old days, the words that made her smile, her song: "I am so fond of you, Marilu." He smells her nighttime odor, mild and slowly rising; he listens to her breathing as she sleeps, and all at once it has become the most important thing in the world.

The rain was pouring in torrents over Port Harcourt when Mr. Rally's chauffeur found a spot for the green V8 on the quay, in front of the offices of the Holland Africa Line, just as Geoffroy had done over a year before to wait for Maou and Fintan to disembark. But this time it was not the *Surabaya* moored to the quay. It was a much bigger, more modern ship, a cargo container ship which did not need to have its rust removed and which was called the *Amstelkerk*. The driver switched off the ignition, and Geoffroy climbed out of the V8, helped by Maou and Fintan. The car no longer belonged to him. A few days earlier he had sold it to Mr. Shakxon, the man who was going to take his place in the offices of the United Africa. At first Geoffroy was indignant: "This is my car, I'd rather give it to Elijah than sell it to that . . . that Shakxon chap!" The Resident intervened, with his gentlemanly politeness. "He'll give you a good price for it, and it will be very useful to him, which means useful to our entire community, don't you see?" Maou said: "If you give it to Elijah, they'll only take it away from him, and he'll get nothing from it. He doesn't even know how to drive." Geoffroy had finally given in, on the condition that Rally handle the transaction and that he be able to use the car in order to get to the ship that was taking them to Europe. The Resident had even offered him his chauffeur: Geoffroy was in no condition to drive.

It had been more difficult with Ibusun. When Shakxon demanded to move into the house straight away, Fintan said: "When we leave, I'll burn it!" But there was nothing for it, they had to leave, and get rid of everything very quickly. Maou had given many things away — chests full of soap, dishes, provisions. In the garden at Ibusun they had organized a sort of party, a bazaar. Maou may have looked jolly, but it was very sad, thought Fintan. As for Geoffroy, he had locked himself away in his study, sorting papers and books and burning his notes as if they were secret archives.

The women, draped in their long robes, stood in line before Marima and Maou. Each departed with a bundle — a saucepan, plates, soap, rice, jam, tins of biscuits, coffee, a sheet, a cushion. Children ran about on the veranda, ducking into the house, pinching things — pencils, scissors. They had cut the ropes of the swing and the trapeze and taken the hammocks away. Fintan was cross. Maou shrugged her shoulders: "Never mind, what does it matter? Shakxon has no children."

By five o'clock that afternoon the party was over. Ibusun was empty, emptier than when Geoffroy had moved in, before Maou's arrival. He was tired. He lay down on the camp bed, the only piece of furniture remaining in his room. He was pale, his gray beard covered his cheeks. With his wire eyeglasses, his black leather shoes on his feet, he looked like an old soldier in confinement. For the first time, Fintan felt something when he looked at him. He wanted to stay by him, to speak to him. He wanted to tell him lies, to tell him they would come back, begin again, and take off on the river to the new Meroë, to the stele of Arsinoë, to the traces left by the people of Osiris.

"Everywhere you go I'll go with you, I'll be your assistant, we'll discover the secrets, we'll be scholars." Fintan remembered the names he had seen in Geoffroy's notebooks — Belzoni, Vivant Denon, David Roberts, Prisse d'Avennes, the black Colossi of Abu Simbel, discovered by Burckhardt. For a moment Geoffroy's eyes shone as when he had seen the sunlight drawing the signs of the *itsi* on the basalt at the entrance to Aro Chuku. Then he fell asleep, exhausted, his face as white as a dead man's, his hands cold. Dr. Charon had said to Maou: "Take your husband to Europe, make him eat. He'll never get better if he stays here." They were leaving. They were going to London, or France, Nice perhaps, to be closer to Italy. They would have a different life. Fintan would go to school. He would have friends his age, he would learn to play their games, to laugh with them, to fight as children do, without touching their faces. He would ride a bike, go skating, eat potatoes and white bread; he would drink milk and fruit syrup, he would eat apples. He would no longer eat dried fish, chili peppers, plantain, and okra. He would forget about *foufou*, roasted yams, and groundnut soup. He would learn to walk with shoes, to cross the street between the cars. He would forget pidgin, he would no longer say: "Da buk we yu bin gimmi a don los am." He would no longer say "Shaka!" to the drunkard staggering along the dusty road. He would no longer call Bony's grandmother, old Ugo, "Nana." She would no longer call him by the gentle nickname he liked so much: "Umu." In Marseilles, Grandmother Aurelia could once again call him "bellino" and give him her strong kisses and take him to the cinema. It would be as if he had never left.

On the last day at Ibusun Fintan went out very early, before sunrise, to run barefoot one last time through the big, grassy plain. Near the termites' castles he waited for the sun to appear. Everything was so vast—the sky washed by rain, marbled by scrolls of clouds. The sound of the gentle wind in the grass, the whirr of insects, the cries of the guinea fowl sheltering somewhere in the trees. Fintan waited for a long time, without moving.

He even heard a snake slide by him in the grass with a slow rasping of scales. Fintan spoke to him out loud, the way Bony used to, "Snake, you're at home here, it's your house, just let me through." He picked up a bit of red earth and rubbed it on his face, on his forehead and cheeks.

Bony didn't come. Since the convicts' uprising he no longer wanted to see Fintan. His older brother and his uncle had been among those Lieutenant Fry's army had shot against the fence. One day they met on the road to Omerun. Bony's face was closed, his eyes unclear beneath his slanting lids. He said nothing, threw no stones, shouted no insults. He went on by, and Fintan felt ashamed. Angry, too, and there were tears in his eyes, because what Simpson and Lieutenant Fry had done was not his fault. He hated them as much as Bony did. He let him walk away. He thought, "If I killed Simpson, could I see Bony again?" Then he went to the white house near the river. He saw the warped fence where the blood had flowed, soaking into the mud. The huge hole of the swimming pool was like a flooded tomb. The water was muddy, blood-colored. There were two soldiers armed with rifles on guard in front of the gate. But the house seemed strangely empty, abandoned. And then Fintan understood that Gerald Simpson would never get his swimming pool. After what had happened no one would come to dig the earth. Every rainy season the big hole would fill up with muddy water; toads would come and sing there at night. That made him laugh, a laugh that was like a revenge. Simpson had lost.

The group of trees at the top of the mound was lonely. From there, Fintan could see the houses of Omerun and all around, the smoke from the other villages rising on the cold morning air. A day like any other was beginning. There was the sound of voices, dogs barking. The high-pitched clanging of a blacksmith's hammer, the dull thudding of pestles crushing the millet. Fintan thought he could smell the fine odor of food being prepared: fried fish, cooked yam, *foufou*. It was the last time. He walked slowly down to the river. The first pier was deserted. The rotten planks were gradually sagging, revealing the blackened pilings choked with grass. Farther down, tied to the wharf, was the boat from Degema, come to collect the yams and plantains, a strange wooden boat which looked like a Portuguese caravel. On waking, Fintan had heard the siren and had given a start. He thought Geoffroy had heard it too: it was the day when the slow mail arrived by river, along with everyday goods. There would be chests of soap to be unloaded in front of the warehouse of the United Africa, and old Moises would drag them over to the shade of the tin roofs. Shakxon might already be there, impatient, pacing back and forth along the wharf, dressed in his impeccable white linen suit (which he changed twice a day), wearing his Cawnpore helmet. The Resident might have come down, too, to greet any visitors, to chat with the captain. Simpson, most certainly, would not be present for roll call. After the riot he had been called to Port Harcourt. The rumor was already afoot that he was going to be sent elsewhere, perhaps called back to London, to sit behind a desk, where he would be less dangerous.

Fintan sat on the ruined pier, looking at the river. Because of the rains the river had risen. The dark, heavy water flowed downstream, creating whirlpools on its way, carrying branches torn from trees, leaves, yellow foam. Sometimes a strange object would float by, come from who knows where—a bottle, a board, an old basket, a rag. Bony said it was the goddess who lived in the river, you could hear her breathe and moan at night, she pulled young men from the shore and drowned them. Fintan thought of Oya, her body sprawled in the dark room, her hoarse breathing at the moment of birth. Fintan had watched the baby come into the world, and he had not dared to move, had not been able to say a thing. Then, when the child had made its first cry, a violent, shrieking cry, Fintan had rushed up on deck to wait for Bony and for help. It was Maou who had gone with Oya to the clinic and who had watched over her. Fintan could not forget how Oya held her child tight against her while they carried her on the stretcher to the hospital. The child was a boy and had no name. Now, Oya had gone away with her son and would never return.

In the middle of the river, at the tip of Brokkedon, the wreck was barely visible. All at once Fintan felt a great apprehension, as if that hull in the river were the most important thing in his life. On the other pier he found a pirogue and pushed himself out into the middle of the river, in the direction of Asaba. Bony had taught him how to paddle by dipping the oar at a slight angle and leaving it a moment alongside the pirogue to keep straight ahead. The water was dark, and the opposite shore was already under the clouds. The electric lights of the sawmill shone among the trees.

It did not take long for the pirogue to reach the middle of the river. The current was powerful, and there was a noise of rushing water around the pirogue; Fintan sensed he was drifting downstream. For a moment he managed to stay on course towards the wreck. The *George Shotton* had begun to sink, just as Sabine Rodes had said it would. It was just a shape, a sort of big, black skeleton arising among the reeds, like the jaw of a sperm whale clenched around the tree trunks that had been carried off by high water, along with the clumps of yellow spume thrown up by the whirlpools. The battering of the uprooted trees had punctured the deck, and water had entered the hull. As the current bore him past the islet, Fintan saw that the stairway that Oya and Okawho had used to climb up had been torn away by the high water. Only the last landing was left, along with the long handrail dipping up and down in the current. Birds no longer nested in the wreck.

At the tip of Brokkedon the pirogue left the channel and entered calm water. Asaba was very near. Fintan could see the quay and the buildings of the sawmill quite clearly. With a heavy heart he turned around to head back to Onitsha. Oya was gone. She was the guardian of the *George Shotton*. Without her the errant tree trunks would destroy everything that remained of the wreck, and the mud would bury it.

In the afternoon, before the rain, Fintan made earthen dolls, one last time, the way he had learned. Bony said, "Make gods." Painstakingly, Fintan made the masks of Eze Enu the sky dweller, Shango the thunder thrower, and the two first children in the world, Aginju and his sister Yemoja, from whose mouth the river water was born. He made soldiers and ghosts and the boats on which they sailed and the houses in which they lived. When he had finished, he put them into the sun to bake, on the cement of the terrace.

In the empty house Maou and Geoffroy were sleeping, in the shuttered room. They were stretched out next to each other on the narrow bed. From time to time they would wake, and Fintan heard their voices, their laughter. They seemed happy.

It was a very long day, an almost endless day, like the day that had preceded Maou and Fintan's departure from Marseilles.

Fintan did not want to rest. He wanted to see everything, to keep everything, for months, for years. Every street in the town, every house, every small shop in the marketplace, the weavers' workrooms, the warehouses at the wharf. He wanted to run barefoot without stopping, as on the day when Bony had taken him to the edge of the void, to the huge, gray stone overlooking the ravine and the valley of the Mamu River. He wanted to remember everything, for his whole life. Every room in Ibusun, every scrape on every door, the smell of fresh cement in the hallway, the rug with the scorpions, the lime tree in the garden, its leaves stitched by ants, the flight of vultures in the stormy sky. Standing on the veranda, he looked out at the lightning. He was waiting for the rumble of thunder, as on the day of his arrival. He could forget nothing.

The rain came. Fintan felt an exhilaration, as on the first days after his arrival. He began to run through the grass, down the slope to the Omerun. In the middle of the prairie were the termite castles, standing like towers of baked earth. In the grass Fintan found a branch broken off during the storm. With a concentrated furor he began to strike the termites' nests. Every blow resounded to the core of his body. He struck the nests, shouting, from deep in his throat, Raaoo, raah, arrh! Segments of wall crumbled, hurling larvae and blind insects into the lethal sunlight. His hands hurt. In his head he could hear Bony's voice telling him, "But these are the gods!"

There was nothing true anymore. At the end of that afternoon, at the end of that year, there was nothing left. Fintan had kept nothing. Everything was lies, just like the stories told to children to make their eyes glow.

Fintan stopped his flailing. He took a bit of the red earth into his hands—a light dust, home to a larva, precious as a gem.

The rain-driven wind blew. It was cold, like nighttime. The sky, over by the hills, was the color of soot. The lightning danced, endlessly.

Sitting on the steps of the veranda, Maou looked over at that same sky. It had been so hot that morning, the sun still burned through the tin roof. There was not a sound outside. Fintan was running through the prairie. Maou knew he would not come back until night. It was the last time. She thought about it without sadness. Now they would have a new life. She could not imagine what it would be like, so far away from Onitsha. What she thought she would miss back there, in Europe, was the gentleness of the women's faces, the children's laughter, their caresses.

Something had changed inside her. Marima had placed her hand on Maou's belly, and she had said the word *child*. She used the pidgin word, *pikni*. Maou laughed, and Marima too began to laugh. But it was true. How had Marima guessed? In the garden, Marima questioned the praying mantis, which is said to know everything about the sex of the child to be born. The mantis had folded its wings onto its chest: "It's a girl," concluded Marima. Maou felt a thrill of happiness. "I'll call her Marima, like you." Marima said, "She was born here." She pointed to the land around them—the trees, the sky, the great river. Maou remembered what Geoffroy had told her, long ago, before leaving for Africa: "People there believe that a child is born the day it is created and that it belongs to the land where it was conceived."

Marima was the only one who knew. "Don't tell anyone." Marima shook her head.

Now Marima had gone. At noon Elijah came to say goodbye. He was going back to his village on the other side of the border, in Nkongsamba. Geoffroy lay on the bed, and Elijah came to squeeze his hands. Outside, Marima waited in the sun in front of the house. She was surrounded by all her luggage—suitcases, boxes full of saucepans. There was even a sewing machine, a fine Triumph, which Maou had bought on the Wharf.

Maou went down and kissed Marima. She knew that she would not see her again, but there was no sadness. Marima took Maou's hands and laid them flat on her belly, and Maou felt that she too was expecting a child. It was the same benediction.

Then a covered lorry came and stopped on the road. Marima and Elijah hoisted their belongings onto the platform, and Marima climbed into the cab, next to the driver. They pulled away in a cloud of red dust.

Before five o'clock the rain began to fall. Fintan was sitting at his favorite spot, on a mound slightly above the great river. He saw the other shore, the dark line of the trees, the red cliffs which looked like a wall. Above Asaba the sky was black, like the hollowed-out darkness of nothingness. The clouds scudded across the treetops, shredding filaments, gliding in a reptilian motion. The river was still lit by the sun. The water seemed immense, the color of mud, shot with gold. The islands rose hesitantly from the water. In the distance was Jersey, surrounded by islets hardly bigger than pirogues. Farther along, at the mouth of the Omerun, lay Brokkedon, tapering and indistinct. The *George Shotton* had probably foundered in the night; there was nothing left. Fintan thought it was better that way. He remembered what Sabine Rodes kept saying about the fall of the empire. Now that Oya and Okawho were gone, everything would change, disappear like the wreck, wash away in the golden alluvium of the river.

In the foreground, just below Fintan, the trees stood out against the light of the sky. The cracked earth was waiting for the storm. Fintan thought that he knew every tree along the edge of the river — the great mango tree with its globular foliage, the thorny bushes, the gray plumes of the palm trees flattened by the north wind. Children were playing on the bare ground in front of the houses.

Suddenly the storm was on the river. The curtain of rain closed over Onitsha. The first drops beat the ground, crackling, raising clouds of acrid dust, tearing leaves from the trees. They scratched Fintan's face, and in an instant he was soaked.

Farther down, children who had hidden reappeared, shouting and running through the fields. Fintan felt a happiness without bounds. He did as the children did. He took off his clothes, and, wearing nothing but his underpants, he ran into the pounding rain, his face lifted to the sky. He had never felt so free, so alive. He ran. He shouted, Ozoo! Ozoo! The naked children, gleaming in the rain, ran with him. They replied, Oso! Oso! Run! Water flowed into his mouth, into his eyes, so abundant that it choked him. But it was good, it was magnificent.

The rain streamed over the earth, blood-colored, carrying everything with it—leaves and branches from the trees, rubbish, even lost shoes. Through the curtain of raindrops Fintan saw the river, immense and swollen. Never had he been so close to the rain, so full of the smell and sound of the rain, which was brimming with the cold wind of the rainstorm.

When he returned to Ibusun, Maou stood waiting for him on the veranda. She seemed angry. Her eyes were hard, almost cruel, and she had a bitter crease on either side of her mouth. "What's the matter?" Maou did not answer. She caught Fintan by the arm, pushed him inside the house. She was hurting him. He didn't understand. "Have you seen the state you're in?" She wasn't shouting, but she spoke harshly. Then all of a sudden she collapsed on a chair. She pressed her hands against her belly. Fintan saw that she was crying.

"Why are you crying, Maou? Are you ill?" Fintan felt sick at heart. He put his hand on Maou's belly.

"I'm tired, I'm so tired. I would like so much to be away, for it all to be over."

Fintan put his arms around her and hugged her very tight.

"Don't cry, it will all be fine, you'll see. I'll always stay with you, even when you're old."

Maou managed to smile through her tears.

In the dim light of the room, Geoffroy's eyes were open. The noise of the storm was growing louder and louder. Lightning illuminated the empty room.

That night, after a hasty meal (a Campbell's soup heated on the gas camping stove, a tin of red beans, biscuits, and the last of the Dutch cheese scraped from the red rind) Maou and Fintan lay down in the same bed in order not to disturb Geoffroy. The grumbling of thunder kept them awake almost until dawn. The green V8 would not be long. Mr. Rally's chauffeur would be there at first light.

Far from Onitsha

Bath Boys' Grammar School, Autumn 1968

Fintan looks at the French class and realizes that he has not forgotten their names, all those names: Warren, Johnson, Lloyd, James, Strand, Harrison, Beckford, Metcalfe, Andrew, Dixon, Mall, Pembro, Calway, Putt, Tinsley, Temple, Watts, Robin, Gascoyne, Goddard, Graham Douglas, Stapilton, Albert Trillo, Say, Holmes, Le Grice, Somerville, Love. When he started at the school, he thought that nothing would have any importance, that it would be a job like any other, just faces, appearances. The boarders' dormitory is a large, cold hall with bars on the windows. Through the windows you can see the trees, set ablaze by autumn. Nothing has changed. It was yesterday, he had just arrived, Geoffroy had driven him to the school, shaken his hand, and left again. And so there were two lives. The one he began to live at school: in the cold dormitory, in the classrooms, with the other boys, Mr. Spinck's nasal whine as he recited verses by Horace, *o lente lente currite noctis equi*; and then there was what he saw when he closed his eyes, in the half-light. Gliding down the Omerun, swinging in the sisal hammock, listening to the sound of the storms.

He had to forget. In Bath no one knew a thing about Onitsha or the river. No one cared a thing about those names which were so important there. When he arrived at the school, Fintan spoke pidgin, inadvertently. He said, "He don go nawnaw, he tok say"; he said, "Di book bilong mi." That made them laugh, and the house master thought he was doing it on purpose to create a stir. He ordered Fintan to stand against the wall for two hours with his arms spread. That too, he had to forget, those words jumping and dancing in his mouth.

He had to forget Bony. At school the boys were both childish and very knowledgeable; they were full of cunning and suspicion and they seemed older than their age. Their faces were pale and unattractive. In the dormitory they spoke in hushed tones, saying things about women's sex organs, as if they had never seen one. Fintan remembers how he looked on the boys at first, with a mixture of curiosity and fear. He could not read their expressions, he did not understand what they wanted. He was like a deaf-mute, watchful, always on guard.

That was a long time ago. Now he is on the side of the masters, a tutor in French and Latin, to make a living. Jenny is a nurse at Bristol hospital. Everyone says they will marry. Perhaps this winter, at Christmas. They plan to go to the area of Penzance, or Tintagel, to be near the sea. When war broke out back there, in Biafra, Fintan wanted to leave straightaway, to try and understand. It is for Jenny's sake that he did not leave. In any case, was there anything he could do? The world he once knew had closed its doors; it was already too late. The mercenaries have signed up for the oil companies—Gulf Oil, British Petroleum—going to Calabar, Bonny, Enugu, Aba. He should never have left, he should have stayed in Onitsha, in Omerun. He should never have let the solitary tree above the grassy plain out of his sight, the place where his friend waited, where adventure began.

But Fintan got used to it. Now, he recalls those one had to avoid, those who could be dangerous. Among the former were James, Harrison, Watts, and Robin. James was their leader. They would go at you in pairs, Harrison grabbing you around the waist, James hitting you with his fist. In the latter group were Somerville, Albert Trillo, Love, and Le Grice. Le Grice was a rather chubby boy, quiet. He planned to

192

be a magistrate, like his father. At fifteen he already looked like a man, with a suit, a scarf, his hair already thinning, and a small moustache.

Love was different. He was a slim, pale boy, stooped, with dark rings under his big eyes and an air of sorrowful languor. The others made fun of him and treated him like a girl. When he came to school for the first time, Fintan felt for him a sort of sympathy mingled with pity. Love talked about other things than women's sex organs. He wrote poetry. He showed some to Fintan, complicated verses about love and regret. There was one poem, Fintan remembers, entitled "One Thousand Years." It was about a soul wandering through a swampland. Fintan thought about Oya, her hiding place on the river, in the wreck. He could not talk about that, either, with anyone.

Now Oya is an old woman, no doubt. And the child born on the river may be among those adolescents with shaved heads, armed with nothing but a stick by way of a rifle, that John Birch saw in Okigwi on his mission for the Save the Children Fund. Fintan scrutinizes the photographs, as if he might recognize Bony's face among the soldiers of Benjamin Adekunle, the "Black Scorpion"—the soldiers confronting the MiG-17s and the Ilyushin-18s, the 105-mm guns in the savannah around Aba. When the war began out there, so far away, it was for Okeke that Fintan wanted to leave—to find him, to help him and protect him, for Fintan was the one who had seen Oya give birth in the belly of the *George Shotton*, he who was like Okeke's brother. Where is he now? Perhaps he is lying in the grass, a hole in his side, on the road to Aba, where thousands of starving children wait, their faces frozen in suffering; they look like little old men. When Jenny looks at the photos in the magazines, she begins to cry. And it is Fintan who must console her, as if he could forget.

Now, he does not know why, it is his memory of Love that surfaces. His eyes, very gentle and luminous; his trembling voice when he read his poems. It was the last year of school. Love had become almost unbearable. He would wait for Fintan at the end of class, taking refuge. His words seemed to cling to Fintan; he was demanding, prickly. He wrote letters to Fintan.

One day Fintan did an unforgivable thing. He joined a group that was bullying Love and slapping him about the face to make him cry. He rejected the boy who had always clung to him, he watched that very tender gaze fill with tears, and he turned away. Afterwards, whenever Love came up to speak to him, Fintan would reply harshly, as Bony had done long ago on the road after the death of his older brother: "Pissop gughe, fool!" Love left the school before the end of the year. His mother came to fetch him. It was the first time Fintan had seen her. She was a very pale and beautiful young woman, with lovely dark hair and with Love's eyes, soft and shining like velvet. She looked at Fintan and he felt ashamed. Love introduced Fintan to his mother, saying: "He has been my only friend here." It was terrible. You had to be hard, never forget what had happened. The memory of the river and the sky, the termites' castles laid bare to the sun, the great field of grass, and the ravines like bleeding wounds—that was what helped you not to fall into the trap, to remain bright and hard, unfeeling, in the manner of the black stones of the savannah, in the manner of the marked faces of the Umundri.

"What are you thinking?" asks Jenny from time to time. Her body is soft and warm; there is the perfume of her hair, close to her neck. But Fintan cannot forget the eyes of the starving children, or the young boys lying in the grass, near Owerri, near Omerun, where he used to run barefoot over the hardened earth. He cannot forget the explosion that destroyed in one instant the column of lorries transporting weapons to Onitsha on 25 March 1968. He cannot forget the charred body of the woman in a jeep, her hand clenched towards the white sky. He cannot forget the names of the pipelines—Ugheli Field, Nun

194

River, Ignita, Apara, Afam, Korokovo. He cannot forget that terrible name: Kwashiorkor.

You had to be hard when Carpet, the Head Boy, pushed you by the shoulders against the schoolyard wall and told you to remove your trousers in order to be caned. Fintan closed his eyes. He thought of the column of convicts crossing the town, the noise of the chain clamped to their ankles. Fintan did not cry, even when the Head Boy beat him; only at night, in the dormitory, biting his lip so he wouldn't be heard. But it was not because of the caning. It was because of the Niger River. Fintan could hear it flowing out there beyond the schoolyard, a slow, deep, gentle sound; he could hear the muffled sound of the storms rolling beneath the clouds, drawing near. In the beginning, when he had just arrived at the school, Fintan would fall asleep thinking of the river, dreaming that he was gliding in the long pirogue, Oya kneeling at the prow, her head turned towards the islands. He would wake up with his heart pounding, the sheets beneath him soaked with a warm liquid. It was shameful; he had to go and wash his sheets himself in the laundry, taunted by the other boarders. But he had never been beaten for that.

And so he had to hold back his dreams, return them to the interior of his body, no longer listening to the song of the river, no longer imagining the rumbling of the storms. In Bath, in the winter, it does not rain. It snows. Even now Fintan is afraid of the cold. In the little room under the eaves on the outskirts of Bristol water freezes in the pitcher. Jenny huddles against him to give him her warmth. Her breasts are soft, and her belly; her voice murmurs his name in her sleep. There is nothing more true or more beautiful on earth, he supposes.

To get to the school to give his classes Fintan has bought an old motorcycle. It is so cold on the way that he has to put newspapers inside his clothes. But Fintan likes to feel the bite of the wind; it is like a knife carving through memories. One becomes naked, like the winter trees.

Fintan remembers when Maou left, autumn 1958. She fell ill in London, and Geoffroy took her away with Marima, to the south. Marima was ten years old; she looked very much like Maou—the same color hair, with glints of copper; the same stubborn forehead, the same eyes catching the light. Fintan was deeply in love with her. He wrote to her nearly every day, and once a week he sent the letters in one big envelope. He told her everything—about his life, his friend Le Grice, the bad tricks they played on Mr. Spinck, about the Head Boy, Carpet, who played the petty dictator; he told her of his plans to escape, to come and join her in the south of France.

Geoffroy had not wanted to return to Nice because of the memory of Grandmother Aurelia. He had never had a family, had never wanted one. Perhaps it was because of Aunt Rosa, whom he despised. After Aurelia's death, the old spinster left to go back to Italy, no one knew where, near Florence, to Fiesole perhaps. Geoffroy bought an old house near Opio. Maou set about raising chickens. Geoffroy found work in an English bank in Cannes. He wanted Fintan to stay in England until the end of his studies, at the boarding school in Bath. As for Marima, she started at a convent school in Cannes. The separation was definitive. When he had finished his studies in Bath, Fintan went on to university at Bristol. To earn a living he accepted a position as French and Latin tutor at the school in Bath, where, oddly enough, the teachers had good memories of his time there.

Now everything has changed. War is erasing memories, devouring the plains of grass, the ravines, the village houses, even the names he once knew. Perhaps there will be nothing left of Onitsha. It will be as if everything had existed only in his dreams, just like the raft carrying Arsinoë and her people to the new Meroë, on the endless river.

196

Winter 1968

Marima, what more can I say, to tell you what it was like, in Onitsha? Nothing remains now of what I knew. At the end of the summer the federal troops entered Onitsha after a brief spell of mortar attacks that caused the last houses still standing at the edge of the river to collapse. From Asaba, the soldiers crossed the river on barges, passing the ruins of the French bridge and the islands submerged by autumn floods. That is where Okeke, the son of Oya and Okawho, was born, twenty years ago now. The barges reached the other shore where the fishing quay used to be, next to the ruins of the wharf and the gutted warehouses of the United Africa. Onitsha was deserted, the houses burning. There were skeletal dogs and, on the heights, women and children with a lost look about them. In the distance, in the fields of grass and along the muddy trails, columns of refugees made their way towards the East, towards Awka, Owerri, Aro Chuku. Perhaps, without realizing it, they passed by the magic castles of the termites, who are the masters of the grasshoppers. Perhaps the sound of their footsteps and their voices woke the great, green snake hidden in the grass, but no one thought to speak to it. Marima, what is left now of Ibusun, the house where you were born — the tall trees where vultures sat, the trails in the dust woven by the ants, and, at the end of the field, on the path to Omerun, the mango tree where Bony used to sit and wait for me?

What is left of Sabine Rodes's house, the large shuttered room with its walls a tapestry of masks, where he locked himself away to forget the world?

197

In the dormitory at school I dreamt that Sabine Rodes was my real father, that it was for his sake that Maou had come to Africa, and that was why she hated him so intensely. I even told her so one day, when I knew she was leaving for France with you and Geoffrey and I said it spitefully, as if everything could be explained away by such madness; I knew that afterwards nothing would be as before. I don't remember what she said—perhaps she merely laughed and shrugged her shoulders. Maou left with you and Geoffrey, for the south of France, and I understood that never again would I see the river or the islands or anything I had known in Onitsha.

Marima, I would like so much for you to feel as I do. Is Africa, for you, no more than a name, a land like any other, a continent one talks about in newspapers and books, a place that is mentioned only because there is a war going on? In Nice, in your room at the university with its angel's name, you are cut off, there is nothing to keep the thread intact. When civil war broke out there, a year ago, and people began to talk about Biafra, you hadn't even a very good idea where it was, you could not understand that it was the country where you were born.

But you must have felt a shiver, a tremor, as if something very old and secret had shattered within you. Perhaps you remembered what I wrote to you one day, for your birthday, in a letter I sent to you from England—that there, in Onitsha, you belong to the land where you have been conceived, and not to the place where you are born. From your room at the university with its fine view of the sea perhaps you looked at the angry sky and thought that the same rain was falling on the ruins of Onitsha.

I would have liked to tell you more, Marima. I would have liked to go there, like Jacques Languillaume, who died at the controls of his Superconstellation, trying to break through the blockade to take medicine and food supplies to the rebels; to be there like Father James in Ututu, so near Aro Chuku. I would have liked to be in Aba as it was besieged, not as a witness but to take the hands of those who were falling, to relieve the thirst of those who were dying. I stayed here, far from Onitsha. Perhaps I did not have the courage, perhaps I did not know how to act, and it was, in any case, too late. For a year I have not stopped thinking about it, not stopped dreaming about everything that has been ravaged and destroyed. The papers, the BBC say little. Bombs, villages razed, children dying of hunger on the battlefields — a few lines, no more. In Umahia, Okigwi, Ikot Ekpene — photos of children blasted by hunger, their faces swollen, their eyes larger than life. Death has a sonorous, terrifying name: Kwashiorkor. That is the name the doctors have given it. Before the children die, their hair changes color, their dried-out skin cracks like parchment. For the sake of control over a few oil wells the world has closed its doors on them — there is no way out through the rivers, the offshore islands, the coast. Only the forest remains, empty and silent.

I've forgotten nothing, Marima. Now, so far away, I can smell the fish frying at the river's edge, I can smell the yams and the *foufou*. I close my eyes and I can taste the sweetness of groundnut soup. And I can smell the smoke as it rises slowly in the evening above the fields of grass, I can hear the children's cries. Must it all disappear forever?

Not for one instant have I lost sight of Ibusun, the grassy plain, the tin roofs baking in the sun, the river with its islands — Jersey, Brokkedon. Even that which I thought I had forgotten has come back to me in the moment of its destruction, like the series of images drowning people are said to see in the instant they lose consciousness. I give it to you, Marima, to you who knew nothing of it, to you who were born of that red earth where the blood now flows and which I know I shall never see again.

Spring 1969

The train moves through the cold night to the south. Fintan has a curious impression of being on holiday, as if he were leaving the depths of winter, and on his arrival the dawn would be warm and humid, full of insect noises and the smells of the earth. On the last ride from Bath to Bristol the road was blocked by drifts. On the grounds of the school the bare trees were stiff with frost. It was so cold that despite the newspapers folded under his clothes Fintan had the feeling that the wind was drilling a hole through his chest. And yet the sky was blue. There was such beauty in that nature, such purity and beauty.

It had all been decided so quickly. Fintan had rung, saying to Maou, automatically, as he always did: "And so how are things?" Maou's voice was strange, choking. She who never wanted to dramatize anything, particularly where Geoffroy's illness was concerned, now said: "Things are not good. He is so weak, he's not eating anymore, not drinking. He's going to die."

Fintan had handed in his resignation to the headmaster. He did not know when he would return. Jenny went with him to the station. She stood very straight on the platform, with her red cheeks, her blue eyes—she truly seemed a fine girl. Fintan was moved; he thought he might not see her again, ever. The train began to pull away; she kissed Fintan very hard, on the lips.

In the night, every time the train clatters over the switches he feels that much closer to Opio. It is the same train he takes every summer to the south to join Marima and Maou, to see Geoffroy again. To measure on their faces the passage of time. Now everything is different. A light fading. Geoffroy is dying.

Fintan thinks of the narrow road which climbs from Valbonne, in the clear light of morning. The house sits perched at the end of a small valley, above the terraced landscape. At the foot of the property is the hen house, now falling into ruin. When Maou first arrived, she built the batteries for the hens and chicks and she had over a hundred. Since Geoffroy fell ill, she has given up, and there are only a dozen or so hens left. Some are old and sterile. Just enough to sell a few eggs to the neighbors. There is also that old, black hen with her ruffled feathers that follows Maou everywhere like a dog, jumping on her shoulder and trying to peck at her gold tooth.

Maou is still beautiful. Her hair is gray, the sun and the wind have etched lines around her eyes and on either side of her mouth. Her hands are callused. She says she has become what she always wanted to be, an Italian peasant. A woman from Santa Anna.

She no longer writes in the afternoon in her school notebooks those long poems that resemble letters. When Maou and Geoffroy left for the south of France with Marima, over fifteen years ago, Maou gave all her notebooks to Fintan in a big envelope. On the envelope she had written the *ninnenanne* Fintan liked so much, the one about Befana and l'Uomo Nero, the one about the Stura bridge. Fintan read all the notebooks, one after the other, for a year. After all this time there are still pages he knows by heart.

It is in one of the notebooks that Fintan learned the secret of Marima's birth—how the praying mantis had announced it, and how she belonged to the river on whose banks she had been conceived. By foraging his memory Fintan had even been able to recall the day it had happened, during the rains.

Geoffroy is lying on the bed, in a room where the shutters are closed against the afternoon light. His face is pale, already hollowed by the approach of death. Sclerosis entered his body long ago, and he can no longer move. He cannot hear the sounds from outside — the wind in the bramble bushes, the sound of dry earth pelting the shutters. Somewhere a plastic tarp is flapping like a wing.

He came home from hospital because there is no hope. His life is slowing down, despite the drip pouring serum into his vein. His life is ebbing from him. Maou is the one who wanted him to come home. She continues to hope, against all reason. She looks at his face, his refined features, the shadows heavy upon his eyelids. His breathing is so faint, it would take so little to extinguish it.

In the morning the nurse comes to help her wash Geoffroy and change the undersheets. She bathes his cuts and his bedsores in a borax solution. His eyes remain closed, his eyelids shut tight. At times a furtive tear takes shape at the inner corner of his eye and hangs from his lashes, shining in the light. His eyes move behind his lids, something steals over his face, a wave, a cloud. Every day Maou speaks to Geoffroy. It has been so long she no longer really knows what she has told him. She has nothing important to say, just talk, that is all. Marima comes in the afternoon. She sits on the cane chair, next to the bed; she also talks to Geoffroy. Her voice is so fresh and young. Perhaps Geoffroy hears her, there, so far away, where his spirit is slipping free of his body. It is like in the old days, in San Remo, when he heard Maou's voice; the music of his vanished happiness. "I am so fond of you, Marilu. . . ."

And even farther, so long ago, as if in another world: the new city, on the islands, in the middle of the amber river. As if in a dream.

Geoffroy glides on the river, carried by the reed raft. He sees the shores covered with dark forests and, all at once, on the edge of the beach, the adobe houses, the temples. It is here, on the shore of the great river, that Arsinoë stopped. The people cleared the forests, opened the roads. Pirogues move slowly among the islands, and fishermen toss their nets among the reeds. Birds fly up into the pale sky of sunrise: cranes, egrets, ducks. The sun's gold disc appears all of a sudden, lighting the temples, lighting the basalt stele on which the sign of Osiris is carved, the eye and the wing of the falcon. It is the sign of the *itsi*, Geoffroy recognizes it, it is carved on Oya's face, the sun and moon on the forehead, the plumes of the wings and tail of the falcon on her cheeks. The sign is blinding, like a shard piercing his pupils to the depths of his body. The stele faces the rising sun, on Brokkedon Island. Geoffroy feels the light entering him, burning him deep within. This then is the truth; only his body kept him from seeing it. Brokkedon, with the wreck of the *George Shotton* like some antediluvian skeleton. The light is very beautiful, dazzling like happiness. Geoffroy looks at the stele and its magic sign, and he sees Oya's face, and everything becomes clear, legible throughout infinite time. The new city of Meroë lies across the two shores of the river, before the island; in Onitsha and Asaba, at the very place where he waited all these years — on the wharf, on the worn floorboards of the United Africa offices, in the sweltering darkness of the warehouses. It is here that the black queen led her people, to the muddy shores where the boats come to unload their crates of merchandise. It is in this place that she erected the stele of the sun, the sacred sign of the Umundri. It is to this place that Oya returned to bear her child. The light of the truth is so powerful that for a moment it illuminates Geoffroy's face, passing over his forehead and his cheeks, a joyous reflection; his entire body begins to tremble.

"Geoffroy, Geoffroy, what is happening?" Maou bends over him, watches him. Geoffroy's face expresses such joy, a burst of light. She gets up from her chair and kneels by the bed. Outside, night is falling upon the hills, a gray, gentle light, the color of the leaves of the olive tree. They can hear magpies jabbering, and the anxious cries of blackbirds. The buzzing of insects swells in the fermenting grass. They can hear the first calls of the toads in the big watertank down the hill. Maou cannot help but think of nighttime as it was then, there in Onitsha: the fear and jubilation it gave her, a shiver along her skin. Every night, since their return to the south, it is the same shiver which reunites her with what has been lost.

In the next room Marima is asleep on the bed with all her clothes on, on the white bedspread, her arm thrown over her face. She is tired from watching over her father the night before. She dreams that Julien, whom Maou mockingly calls her "fiancé," is taking her on his motorcycle along the shady roads to the sea. Marima is still so young, Maou did not want her to stay, to have to go through all this. Yet Marima wants to cook, to help with bathing her father, with washing the undersheets and the bed linen. She talks all the time of Fintan, who is due to arrive at any moment, as if everything would change when he arrived. Maou thinks: "Do we bring children into the world so that they can close our eyes?"

In the room, Maou has got up again. She no longer dares to speak. She watches Geoffroy's face, his eyes, where his fine lids tremble as if they were at last going to open. One instant more, and the heat and light pass, on the other side of his eyelids, like a reflection upon water.

The sun illuminates the walls and ramparts of the city, the island temples, the black stone bearing the magic sign. It is far away, it is strong and strange, at the heart of Geoffroy Allen's dream. Then the light fades. Shadow enters the little room, covering the face of the dying man, sealing his eyelids forever. The desert sand has covered the bones of the people of Arsinoë. The road to Meroë has no end.

Fintan arrives shortly before nightfall. Everything is so calm in the old house perched at the top of the hill, with just the sound of the wind in the bramble bushes and the heat of the sun still seeping from the walls. It is so far from everything, outside time. In front of the door, in the light of the electric bulb, the old, ruffled hen is chasing moths with the gestures of an insomniac.

Maou kisses Fintan. She has no need to speak, he understands what has happened as he looks into her ravaged face. He goes into Geoffroy's room and feels something shift in his heart, as it did long ago, before they left Onitsha. Geoffroy's face is very white, very cold, with an expression of gentleness and peace that Fintan has never seen. The wind has dropped. It is a night like any other, beautiful and calm. You can already feel the spring. Outside, insects whir madly, and the toads have started up their refrain in the watertank.

In the next room, Marima sleeps deeply on the narrow bed, her head to one side, her brown hair slipping over her shoulder. She is beautiful.

Fintan sits down on the floor, next to Maou, in the room full of shadows. Together they listen to the joyful echo of insects' cries.

It is all over. In Umahia, Aba, Owerri the famished children no longer have the strength to hold their weapons. In any case, against the planes, against the guns, they had nothing left but sticks and rocks. At Nun River, at Ugheli Field, the technicians have repaired the pipelines and the ships will be able to fill their tanks at Bonny Island. The entire world has looked away. Only the oracle of Aro Chuku, by some mysterious agreement, has not been destroyed by bombs.

Some weeks before deciding to leave the school for good and return to the south, Fintan received a letter from a solicitors' office in London. Just a few words informing him that Sabine Rodes had met his death during a bombing raid in Onitsha, at the end of the summer of 1968. He had left instructions for Fintan to be notified of his death. The letter went on to say that his real name was Roderick Matthews, and that he was an Officer of the British Empire.

Printed in the United States
126357LV00002B/1-138/P